Corvid's Lament

ABIGAIL WEEKES-LOWE

Michael Terence
Publishing

First published in paperback by
Michael Terence Publishing in 2017
www.mtp.agency

Copyright © 2017 Abigail Weekes-Lowe

Abigail Weekes-Lowe has asserted her right to be identified as
the author of this work in accordance with the
Copyright, Designs and Patents Act 1988

This book is a work of fiction. Neither the words spoken by the
characters nor the actions taken by them should be attributed
to any real-life persons, living or dead. Any resemblance is
purely coincidental

ISBN 9781973217824

All rights reserved. No part of this publication may be
reproduced, stored in a retrieval system, or transmitted, in any
form or by any means, electronic, mechanical, photocopying,
recording or otherwise, without the prior permission of the
publishers

Cover image
Copyright © rudall30

Cover design
Copyright © 2017 Michael Terence Publishing

Corvid's Lament

ABIGAIL WEEKES-LOWE

For my mother Rose, my husband Denis and my daughter Rebecca.

And for my father Rene and brother Stuart both of whom died far too young.

Prologue

Corvid laments from high above,
Corvid does not hate,
Corvid does not love.

Corvid performs his tasks without a care,
Corvid is invincible,
he has nothing to fear.

Corvid is eternal,
Corvid is free.
Corvid alone knows the destiny,
the destiny of humanity.

Chapter 1

While our house was being built, we lived in rented accommodation. It was a lovely house, but it was adjacent to a cemetery. Looking out of the back windows of all the bedrooms, all you could see was green grass interrupted by rows and rows of graves. Crows flew in circles above the cemetery and invariably perched on the headstones. Their presence gave the cemetery a sinister feel. Daddy said every time he looked out of the window it reminded him of Alfred Hitcock's film The Birds. There was one really large black bird with a turkey neck. There was something almost human about it. Mummy said it was a vulture and Daddy said it was a Corbeau. Its red rimmed eyes were piercing and menacing, like a human soul looked out from it. Daddy was petrified. He has been brought up to be superstitious and definitely believed in Obeah, black magic, and evil spirits. We all thought it was a bit funny, a grown man being so scared of spirits. Daddy pretended not to be scared but we all knew he was.

Dad was clever, he was a lecturer but he missed his real vocation in life, to be a lawyer. When a new law came out in Trinidad protecting tenants from rising rents for three years, providing they registered their tenancy within a three month deadline, Dad was first in line and registered our tenancy straight away. That done, our landlord was prevented from raising our rent for three years. It seemed Mr Sam Ramlochan our landlord was ignorant of the new law.

A few months later myself and my two brothers Ben and Toby were playing on the Veranda, when Mr Ramlochan stormed up the stairs. Mum was hanging out the washing.

Mr Ramlochan looked mad vex, his eyes were bulging with rage. He bellowed at Mum "where's your bastard husban". Mum was visibly shocked, Mr Ramlochan had previously always been so polite.

"Calm down what's happened" Mum said.

Mr Ramlochan bellowed "your bastard husban' gone an' register the rent behind meh back , now I can't kick you out the damn house and I can't put up yuh rent, ...he do all this behin me back - the bastard".

At this point Dad came out on the Veranda with a cricket bat. Dad always kept a cricket bat and a cutlass under the bed for security. Dad said "what's all this shouting about, we didn't do anything wrong, we only did what we were within our rights to do".

Mr Ramlochan shouted "you feel you is a big man eh! Yuh come out here with cricket bat for meh, eh heh?!"

Dad looked at the cricket bat in his hand and seemed to reflect on the absurdity of the situation. Dad sighed, put the cricket bat down on the floor and sat down on one of the Veranda chairs, he paused looked down and then looked up at Mr Ramlochan.

When Dad spoke, his voice was steady "look Sam sit down, let's discuss this amicably".

Mr Ramlochan was silent for a while and the air seemed pregnant with a temporary calm.

I thought to myself, thank God let's hope it all calms down.

I looked up at Mr Ramlochan and a heightened tension gripped my body.

His body began to twitch, his face twisted into a rage, his eyes bulged, he looked like he was going to explode. At the top of his voice he screamed

"amicably, am ic,,,,ab...ly".

Ben and Toby's eyes widened with shock and Toby bit his lip and began to cry.

Mr Ramlochan continued "you think you is a big educated man and I is a damn fool! Why you don't take your 'am ic...ab...ly' and shove it down your throat so you can choke on your big big words! And while you are at it, you can kiss my big black arse! Don't worry I'm not finished with you!" and with that Mr Ramlochan stormed down the stairs.

We were all mortified at what had just occurred, on what was, moments before a peaceful Sunday afternoon. Mum comforted Toby. Dad visibly shaken, said he felt Mr Ramlochan's last remark constituted a threat and to be on the safe side he would report the incident to the police the next day. The incident stayed with us like a stain on a previously blank canvass, but no one mentioned it again.

A few days later - after school, we were just settling down to do our homework, when we heard a loud banging at the door. Dad opened the door and there stood Mr Ramlochan and his two adult sons. Mr Ramlochan looked red and unsteady on his feet, he was clearly drunk. He shouted "you really is a bastard boy, yuh report me to the police eh! You think you is so so clever".

Dad ran into the bedroom and grabbed the cricket bat. Toby immediately began to cry. Ben ran out into the veranda and mimicking Dad, ran back in with his cricket bat poised to strike.

Dad had turned crimson and shouted "I will whip your

backsides raw, if you don't get out of my house now".

Mr Ramlochan said "you mistake my house for yours, yuh stupid arse! I'm the landlord boy".

Dad shouted back "yeah well it's my house for the next three years while I carry on paying the rent".

Mr Ramlochans's sons lunged forward as if to attack Dad, but Mr Ramlochan despite his inebriated state, turned to them and held up his hands to stop them.

He then turned back to Dad, his face twisting into an evil smirk, and he said in a slow calm voice "doh worry we aren't going to attack yuh, but you mark my word, he who laughs last, laughs the best! I will fix you boy, I will fix you good and proper, you'll will be laughing on the other side of your face soon!"

Before Dad could respond Mr Ramlochan and his sons turned around and ran back down the stairs.

The silence that ensued was tangible; there was something sinister in Mr Ramlochan's words that seemed to hit a nerve with all of us. A cold feeling enveloped my body and Mum began to cry. Dad put on a brave face, he cuddled Mum and said "don't worry with him Serena, can't you see the man is a drunkard! He's a fool, he's just bigging up himself, grand standing and making empty threats".

I looked at Dad as he cuddled Mum, but there was no bravado in his eyes, just fear!

Chapter 2

School in the week, beach every Saturday and church on Sunday ...Life settled back down into a normal routine after that and we forgot all about that unpleasant incident.

Life was sweet Mayaro beach, Maracas beach, Las Cuevas beach... a different beach every weekend.

At the beginning of the long six week school break, we always rented a large beach house on Mayaro beach and shortly after the incident with Mr Ramlochan, that is exactly what we did. It felt good to throw off the shackles of the school books and homework and kick back. Ben and Toby were ecstatic Ben couldn't dump his school bag down fast enough and Toby took his time agonising about which toys he should pack for the trip.

Mum and Dad packed the car and then we all jumped in for the two hour drive to the beach house.

When we arrived, my aunts, uncles and cousins had already arrived. The music was blasting out loud and the barbeque had been started. As soon as we arrived we ran to view our bedrooms. I was sharing with my girl cousins Shanti and Ruby and Ben and Toby were sharing with Kelvin and Harry. There was endless food being cooked by the adults, peas and rice, stew chicken, macaroni pie, pig foot sous, callaloo and crab, washed down by endless rum and coke and coconut water.

For us children, all we had to do was eat and play and bathe in the warm sea. The sand was warm and golden under our feet and Toby laughed as he dug his toes in as he walked along. Harry and Kelvin decided to build sand castles and Toby decided to bury Ben's entire body with sand. When Toby was finished all we could see was Ben's head.

Shanti, Ruby and I, jumped in the water and immediately began chatting about the most fashionable swimsuits, as we admired other girls and women on the beach. Shanti giggled "did you see dem two girls walking by just then, OMG half their backsides was hanging out their pants, someone should tell dem they aint cool and they should put those wobbly bum cheeks away". We all exploded in fits of laughter. Ruby said "I want to get some tight hot pants, I will look hot, hot, hot in them with my figure". I promptly remembered a magazine article I read that the white hot pants were the most in fashion and I proceeded to tell them all about it with some authority. Ruby said, "I don't know what your magazine article says, but I aint convinced, I'm sticking with my plan I'm going to get red hot pants to go with my red stiletto heels".

Suddenly Shanti looked serious and said "you all I have something to tell you" she paused and looked a bit sheepish "I start my periods and Mum said now I have to be careful cos now I could get pregnant if I play around with boys". Ruby started to giggle and she blurted out "how you get periods already when yuh breasts flat like pancake!" Shanti's face flushed with shame and she looked down at her flat chest.

Ruby smiled and looked down at her vast chest and said "my boobs is big and firm and I aint got no periods yet". Ruby continued "you see how my bum shape nice, my stomach flat, right now the boys are going mad for me, and I tell you something I am making the most of it".

Shanti looked thoughtful and said "all the boys does say you have a good figure Ruby and you know it, so you lucky, you could fool around with boys all yuh like til yuh periods come".

Ruby continued "You remember Paul from my village, that red skin boy with the lovely smile and big muscles, well he said he'd let me feel his sausage if I let him see my big blubbers- those are his words not mine!" - she laughed

I was shocked and horrified but Shanti started to giggle. Shanti squealed "are you going to do it Ruby?"

Ruby looked thoughtful and twirled her hair "I'm not sure but I'm thinking about it".

Suddenly, maybe because of my shocked silence both girls then focussed on me, I could see them eyeing my petite frame. I felt disgusted by them, they seemed like loose girls who fooled around with boys. I realised that I had nothing in common with them really; we were on different pages, they were not in my social class at all.

I had no intention of discussing menstruation issues with them, especially as I had nothing to say, I seemed to be a late developer in that department and I still had the body of a child, at least Shanti had little humps even if they were like mosquito bites!

I looked at them up and down and before they could say anything I said "I don't fool around with boys so it's not relevant". They both looked at each other and burst out laughing. Shanti looked at me in a pitying way and said "girl you is an uptight little thing, let your hair down and have some fun".

After that we all went quiet, wrapped in our own thoughts, we bobbed up and down in the water, dodging the foaming waves, it felt so serene as the warm turquoise sheets of water washed over us. I floated on my back and watched the cloudless sky, I could feel the heat of the sun scorching my skin. After a while we could hear music wafting along the beach becoming louder and louder as it got closer. It was my older cousin Ronald in his brand new maxi taxi. He pulled up on the beach the music blaring from his car speakers. All the boys ran towards him, he had brought sweets and was sharing them out. Toby and Ben were jumping up and down trying to catch the bags of sweets, as Ronald threw them randomly all around. Kelvin caught the first bag of sweets and Ronald shouted "looks like we have a cricketer in our midst!"

We girls stayed in the water bobbing up and down to the sway of the waves, Ruby sighed wistfully and said "I love this song". I listened carefully to the song blaring out of the speakers and could hear Leo Sayer singing "Oh Oh, Yea Yea, I love you more than I can say". "I love it too" I said and then in tandem we all shouted out "I'll love you twice as much tomorrow, Oh love you more than I can say". We sang along happily to the rest of the lyrics and the tune played over and over in my head, long after it had finished playing.

After lunch, Uncle Marlon climbed the coconut tree and we sat around the tree while he burst each coconut with his cutlass. Ben whispered playfully to me and Toby "oh that sweet flesh of the coconut, washed down by the sweet coconut water" and Toby chirped "yum yum yum". Then Toby stood up and shouted, "Mum can we have some mangoes". Dad shouted back "which one you want Doudouce mango or Julie mango?" Toby shrugged his shoulders and shouted back "either" and then moved his hips sideways and did a little jig. My heart filled with love for my little brother, he was so cute in his spider man bathing trunks.

Then Dad shouted "ice cream!"

Dad's homemade ice cream was the best. Toby shouted back "don't forget the sparkles".

As Mum dished up the ice cream she hummed happily as she sprinkled little sparkly edible balls and hundreds and thousands on top of each bowl. As we all tucked into the creamy vanilla and coconut ice cream, Toby said "I love the sparkles best".

Ben corrected "they are not sparkles, they are sprinkles!"

Ruby giggled and said "you are both wrong they are not sparkles or sprinkles, they are magic bits of glitter, melt the glitter on your tongue and make a wish!"

I huffed "Ruby stop talking rubbish!"

Ruby eyed me up and down, she looked at Shanti and gave a knowing nod. Then she looked at me again and said in her bitchy little voice "Connie lighten up, you absolute nerd!" Everyone collapsed in fits of laughter, including me, it was too nice a day to hold grudges.

Later the sky turned a slightly darker hue and we could feel light rain drops brush our skin. "It's raining" I shouted with glee "let's all have a warm bath"". We children all raced toward the sea and jumped in and as we did the rain started to fall a bit harder. The rain was like a warm shower, bathing us with refreshing droplets. We all squealed with delight. Ben, Toby and I held hands and danced inside the waves, together. As the heavens opened, the rain created a waterfall over us and seemed to cocoon us in our own mini whirlpool. I looked up at the heavens and shouted over the rain "this is the life!" Ben and Toby smiled at me and nodded "this is the life" they both screamed over the sounds of the rain and waves.

At that point life was perfect nectar, a happy carefree life in beautiful Trinidad.

Chapter 3

Some say, happiness is just a small wave which emerges now and then, in an endless sea of sorrow and our sorrow was about to usurp that wave of happiness.

Just before the new term started a swarm of blue bottle flies flew into our house and landed all over the living room. They were on the ceiling, on the walls and all over the windows. They looked like they had been glued on, their blue green bodies and opaque black wings made my blood crawl. I'd never seen anything like it, before or since. We all sprayed with fly spray, and swiped at them, Dad even tried to brush them off with a long-handled broom. But nothing worked, the flies held on to all surfaces buzzing away for several hours. We were all terrified. Then the big vulture Corbeau bird appeared at our living room window and as if they had been commanded, the flies all flew out of the house. It was a weird experience that happened and was over and that none of us spoke about again.

One night a few months after that, Dad woke up in the middle of the night shouting. The three of us jumped out of bed and ran into Mum and Dad's room. Dad was sweating profusely and shouting "something has just jumped into my body! Something has just jumped into my body!"

Mum was trying to calm him down. "Harry darling" she was saying "you have just had a nightmare, come on calm down, you are scaring the kids". Dad was wide eyed, he looked at Mum and then he looked at the three of us in turn. His face contorted with fear, his eyes watered and tears spilled over onto his cheeks. I was shocked, I'd never seen Dad cry before.

"No" Dad whispered "I'm telling you the truth, something just jumped into my body. It's still in there I can feel it".

Every night after that, Dad woke up sweating profusely and shivering. The doctors put it down to a bad case of flu, gave Dad some antibiotics and we all carried on as usual. But Dad didn't get any better. One day at school Mum came to collect us early; she said Dad had collapsed at work and had been rushed to hospital.

Dad said they suspected malaria or yellow fever but the tests for those came back negative. They tested for HIV, hepatitis, cancer, lupus and a host of other illnesses; they did biopsies and prodded and poked Dad and gave him a range of medications. Professors came and examined Dad's notes and they gave their opinions. But despite these interventions and tests, night after night Dad woke up sweating and shaking.

Dad tried to put a brave face on it at first but we could see he was scared. One day just before visiting hours was up, Dad turned to Mum and said "Serena do you think I'm going to die?" Dad's face was thin and ashen so the whites of his eyes seemed huge. Mum didn't answer, her bottom lip started to wobble and Ben quickly patted Dad on the shoulder and said "of course you are not going to die, Dad".

As we walked out of the hospital Mum said quietly "do you think Sam Ramlochan did something to your Dad?"

"Oh my God" blurted Ben "Mum don't be so ridiculous, there are no evil spirits!" I looked at Toby's frightened little face, I took his hand and gave him my brightest smile but I wasn't smiling inside.

We continued to visit Dad every day with Mum, even on school days. Every day we could see Dad was becoming weaker and weaker. Soon he was bed ridden, too weak to get up and he developed large blue black pustules all over his back and legs. The doctors said these were called bedsores or pressure ulcers. Soon Dad was screaming out in pain as these bedsores eventually burst, oozing black blood.

One night Dad's breathing slowed and his eyes shut tight and he could not be awoken.

We got called into the relative's room in the middle of the night, the doctors said Dad had slipped into a coma, he had developed septicaemia which had lead to multiple organ failure. They couldn't identify the cause of the constant high fever, there was nothing more they could do - it was like a car going downhill without the brakes on.

Mum screamed when she heard that news - she went back to the ward and collapsed onto a chair at the side of Dad's bed. She held on to Dad's hand and rocked gently back and forth with her head bent forward, emitting a low humming cry - she stayed like that for several days not moving from Dad's side until he slipped away. The three of us felt both helpless and useless as we watched on.

I will never forget the last breath Dad took. He just stopped breathing abruptly. I imagined his soul exiting his body because he immediately seemed flatter all at once, sort of deflated.

His face was no longer contorted with pain, he looked youthful and serene. His mouth was slightly ajar in a kind of half smile and I remembered thinking quite randomly, what a waste of perfectly good white teeth.

The last breath he took was both extremely traumatic and at the same time a huge relief. It was traumatic for obvious reasons, but the relief experienced was unexpected and felt wrong. It was relief at the cessation of suffering both for him and for us, the cessation of endless journeys to hospital. The cessation of endless tests, the cessation of endless hope, which deep down we had all known was hopeless.

Chapter 4

After Dad died, Mum went to pieces and life for me and my two younger brothers was never the same again.

Mum tried to keep on working but her wages were not enough to keep up the rent on the house we were living in, plus continue to finance the new house we were building. Dad had died without adequate life insurance. To be fair he was only forty-eight and probably wasn't worried about life insurance at that age. Mum tried to carry on as usual taking us to school, making us dinner, doing the laundry etc but it all soon got on top of her. She'd breakdown and cry often and take to her bed for days.

For several months, relatives came to visit, various aunts and sometime uncles came to stay to help out. Shanti's Mum and Ruby's Mum came to stay for extended periods and at one point Ruby and Shanti came too. They said they were really sorry about our Dad dying, but they didn't act very sad. Ruby was forever reapplying her red lip gloss and Shanti, Ruby's little lapdog, was still pandering to Ruby's every need.

One-day Ruby was wearing a tight red boob tube and red hot pants, her hair was nicely waved and her red lips were pouty. There was no denying she was pretty, but in that moment I hated her. I barged past her and said "Ruby do you really think you are dressed appropriately to visit a death house?" Ruby narrowed her eyes at me and replied "what happen you jealous you could never look this good?" Shanti who was looking on, giggled hysterically.

A few days later I saw Ruby cosying up to Ben in the living room. She was sitting close to him thrusting her large breasts towards him. I crept nearer to the door and heard her say "Ben you is one good looking boy, have you ever popped a girl's cherry?"

I was looking forward to Ben pushing her away, but instead he flashed her one of his cheeky grins. I was appalled, I pushed my way into the room and said "Ruby are you so desperate for attention that you are flirting with your own cousin, when his father has just died?"

Ruby stood up straight, flicked her hair and put her hands on her waist, she opened her mouth to say something but before she could, I shouted "be careful you will be buying nappies soon" and I slammed the door.

As time passed, eventually the relatives had to go back to their own families and we were left alone again. I tried to help as much as I could and largely took over caring for Toby. Ben was mostly self sufficient.

I don't know how it started but eventually Mum found solace in white rum. Initially she just sat drinking and crying alone, but after a few weeks she seemed to acquire drinking mates and Ben, Toby and I began to dread what we'd come home to after school. Sometimes Mum was happy surrounded by her drinking buddies, music boomed from the house and she pranced about in flouncy dresses or carnival costumes to the latest Soca tunes. Sometimes she would play tabanca love songs and sob along to the words with a box of tissues at the ready. At other times she was inconsolable, the house a total mess, no shopping bought, no food cooked for us and she took to her bed. We were never disciplined, no one imposed any boundaries on us or made us do our homework, or made us brush our teeth, because no one cared.

Nevertheless, we were scared: - scared of what scenario

would greet us when we opened the front door. I dreaded every scenario equally and I think Ben felt the same. Toby however was happy when Mum seemed happy. She'd often grab him to dance as we came through the front door and still in his uniform, he held her hand and danced with her and her friends, blissfully unaware that they were all totally inebriated.

Ben and I were constantly on high alert. Ben had to stop one of Mum's female friends, on two occasions trying to encourage Toby to drink punching rum.

One day as we came home from school, Mum was in a drunken stupor on the settee. Mum's rasta mate Selassi was in the kitchen, he stunk of ganja. As soon as I entered the kitchen and before I could react Selassi grabbed my arm hard and pulled me towards him. I screamed and pulled away but not before he planted a slobbery wet kiss on my cheek. Ben who was behind me, quickly pulled Selassi off me and shoved him aggressively out of the way. Selassi already unsteady from drink, went flying across the room, hitting his head hard on the terrazzo floor. Selassi remained motionless; we both thought he was dead. For several hours Ben and I were nervous wrecks, my heart pounded and my head throbbed, on two occasions Ben ran to the toilet to throw up. Every time Mum looked like she was waking up we panicked, thinking about how we were going to explain the dead body on the kitchen floor. Luckily for us Toby wasn't at home as he was staying with a friend.

After several hours Ben and I contemplated calling the police but we worried that the police seeing Mum and the house in such a state, might take us into care. Just as we were reviewing our options, Selassi woke up and in slow motion stood up unsteadily, revealing a large gash at the back of his head, he opened the front door and staggered out. We never saw him again.

When Toby came home the next day he said he'd seen an ambulance, Ben and I took no notice until Toby continued "I heard someone say Selassi died of a head injury".

When Mum came out of her bedroom that morning she looked pale and worried. "Mum what's wrong" said Toby running towards her.

Mum sank into a chair and lit a cigarette slowly, her eyes were wide, she opened her mouth as if to speak but then closed it again, she gazed into space, finally she spoke:

"Someone got into the bed with me last night, at first I thought it was you Toby coming in for a little cuddle. But then I got a strong whiff of ganja and I knew it was Selassi. I turned around to ask him what the hell he was doing in my bed, but when I turned to look at the bed bedsides me, there was no one there, except I could sense a physical presence next to me, but I couldn't see anything. I tried to scream but a silent agonised cry came out of my mouth. Then I heard a noise and I looked up and I saw that blasted vulture looking at me through the window. I got so scared, I said the Hail Mary and asked God to protect us".

Ben looked at me his eyes round and gulped, then he said with a false exuberance "Mum you've been drinking too much rum again!"

Ben and I never discussed the incident again but developed a tacit understanding. We continued as substitute Mum and Dad, finding us some cereal or bread for breakfast and whatever else we could find to eat after school. Sometimes Mum surprised us and remembered to go shopping but mostly it became a chaotic existence of scrounging around for food and trying to avoid Mum's new loud and vulgar friends. Mum was so oblivious to everything, I don't think she ever missed Selassi. The whole situation was unsustainable and my heart yearned for the home life which we had previously enjoyed, but which now seemed like a lifetime ago.

After a while gossip spread like wildfire about the drunkard widow Serena, who was having wild parties with waste of space drunkard men and whose children were running wild and scrounging around for food.

Soon the rumours reached Granny Betty, Dad's Mum and one day after school we came home to a screaming match between Granny Betty and Mum.

Mum said Granny was an old witch who lacked any emotion, she sobbed she didn't want her kids being cared for by someone who had no feelings. Mum screamed "you don't have a nurturing bone in your body". Granny on the other hand, called Mum a disgrace, a terrible Mother, an intoxicated tart, who cared more about the inside of a bottle of rum than her own kids. After more and more screaming Gran calmly said "look Serena I leave this house with all three children or I call Social Services - the choice is yours".

Mum looked around at the filthy house strewn with empty cups and rum bottles, she paused and looked at us all in turn. She stayed like that trance-like for a while, then she called us to her and snuggled us in her arms, she cuddled us tight. Suddenly she let go and sat heavily on a chair, her shoulders heaved and she collapsed in sobs. Eventually she whispered, "kids go and pack your bags you are going to live with Granny".

Ben and I packed in stunned silence, while Toby hugged Mum around her neck and wept.

Chapter 5

It was a relief in a way to move to a calm and stable environment with Granny but we did miss Mum and the life we had before Dad died. Living with Gran brought stability to our lives again, she fed us and clothed us, made sure we brushed our teeth, did our homework and went to school.

But Granny was a staunch Catholic and she lived in accordance with the scriptures. She told us that we had to always be on our best behaviour because God is always watching us and always knows what we do wrong. Granny said that God could see all our actions; he could hear all the bad things we said, and he knew when we told lies. Every night before bed Granny made us sit down as a family to say the Lord's prayer, the Hail Mary and the 23rd Psalm.

We went to church every Sunday with Gran and often she went to church on her own during the week on feast days and holy days. She even went to a rosary group too. Gran made us stay after church on Sunday to go to the children's bible group. There we discussed bible stories and drew pictures and wrote stories and it was generally fun. Ben and I were in the older bible group and Toby was in a bible class with the younger children. It was here that I met my best friend Martha, who was also in my class at school. Ben and Toby made friends too which was good as most of the children in bible group also went to our new school.

After bible group we would run home to Gran, who always had a big Sunday lunch waiting for us. During lunch Gran would test us on what we had learned during the bible class. After Sunday lunch she always had our school uniforms washed and starched ready for Monday morning.

Gran allocated set chores for us all. Toby had to clean his room and put away the dishes. Ben had to clean his room, keep the veranda and yard clean and swept and he had to make sure the latrine was maintained. I had to clean my own room, clean the living room and wash the dishes after each meal.

Everything was ordered with Gran, spick and span and proper. She always told us that as her grandchildren we had to conduct ourselves "proper".

Unfortunately, though, there was something about Gran that was missing- the warm and cosy bit that we had at home with Mum and Dad, that is what was missing. Gran was not warm and cosy, she was hard and cold. It was like she had never learned how to show love and kindness. Not that she was unkind all the time, she was just kind of stoic, devoid of emotion. She was pragmatic and functional and there was no deviating from that.

She wasn't used to the chatter of children in her home and we were not allowed to chat freely. When she was in, we would have to sit quietly and read. Not being able to speak, we'd take a chance and whisper to each other when Gran wasn't looking. But more often than not, we'd often write and pass secret notes to each other to communicate. Toby and I towed the line without question, but as time went by I could sense that Ben was getting frustrated by having his wings clipped so much at home.

One night after prayers, when Gran was going on about how God knows everything, Toby looked at Gran and asked "does God know what we are thinking Granny?

Gran pointed her fingers at all of us and said "don't

think you all can fool God you know, he has eyes and ears everywhere and God knows all your thoughts, so don't think you can outsmart him".

Toby and I were frightened of Granny but Ben burst out laughing "don't be ridiculous Gran" he said "sometimes bad thoughts just pop into people's heads, we can't control our every thought, even you can't control your thoughts Gran".

Gran's face turned stony she picked up the bible and waved it at Ben, she shouted in her tinny hoarse voice "Proverb 22 says - he who sows wickedness reaps trouble".

Ben turned away and laughed "whatever Gran" he smirked. Gran eyed Ben with a dark look that made me shudder.

Every weekend Gran went out to the market to buy food and provisions for the week and during those times the three of us messed about, shouted, sang and spoke freely.

One weekend when she came back from the market she looked sterner than usual. That night after our prayers Gran said that our cousin Shanti had done wickedness and had reaped trouble. "Oh no" said Toby "what did she do?" Gran paused for effect and responded "she entered the path of sin with a village layabout and now she come home with a big belly. She's ruined her life, she's only eighteen". Toby looked concerned and asked, "Gran how did she get a big belly". Gran pausing for effect again said, "she let Satan lead her away from the right path". Toby looked down at his hands and then looked up, but before he could ask another question Ben said "Toby, Shanti had sex with a boy and now she's pregnant".

Granny gasped a loud painful gasp "Ben" she shouted

"you little heathen don't use those vulgar words under this roof".

Ben hesitated but then stood up, and went over to Gran, he now towered over her, he looked down on Gran, put his hand on Gran's shoulder and said "Granny Betty, Toby is twelve years old, if you want us to understand what you are saying, you have to speak to us in God's plain English". Ben kissed Gran on the top of her head and said "goodnight Gran".

Gran looked at Ben her eyes narrowed and her mouth wide, gaped open.

A few months later Gran came home angry, she said she'd heard that Ben had been flirting with the girl Sarah whose parents owned the sweet shop. Gran shouted at Ben "look Ben I know you think you know everything, but that girl's mum, Lorna, is a La Diablesse and for all you know her daughter Sarah might be one too".

Toby as usual piped up "what's a La Diablesse?"

I had heard the word but didn't know what it meant, Ben and I looked at each other and shrugged.

Gran looked at us in turn and said "Oh Lord you kids don't know nothing, this is really important for you all to know, sit down and listen. This is really serious, listen good".

As instructed we all sat down and Gran started...

"Lorna comes from a French family. A long time ago one of Lorna's female ancestors was pregnant. She was very beautiful with long flowing hair and she was very happily married. Her life was perfect in every way. But as the lady was about to give birth, her husband died unexpectedly. This lady was crushed and was so overcome by grief that she committed suicide during pregnancy by drowning herself. After she died she came back as a Churile spirit. Her long hair was untied and all messed up and streamed all over her face, she dressed in a long white dress and carried her foetus in her arms. Sometimes in the dead of the night if you listen carefully you can hear her, she wails sorrowfully as her unborn child cries for milk. They say the unborn child of a Churile sounds like a cat crying. The Churile who was in eternal grief for her lost child sought out all the pregnant women she could find. Out of envy she possessed them and took away the babies in their womb. They say all miscarriages are the work of the Churile.

When Lorna's grandmother was pregnant the Churile wanted her baby, but Lorna's grandmother was in touch with the spirit world. She begged the Churile and the spirit world to let her keep her baby, promising to do anything in return. The spirit world agreed, Lorna's grandmother was born human but she agreed to make a pact with the devil to become a demon, a La Diablesse. Lorna's grandmother kept her baby, but became a female devil. Outwardly she still seemed human and absolutely beautiful but she always wore a long dress which hid the fact that one leg ends in a cow's hoof. Lorna's grandmother promised the devil that all her female relatives would become devil women, as long as they could bear and keep their children. Lorna's mum is therefore a La Diablesse and so is her daughter Sarah. Don't you see how they always wear trousers or long dresses, so you can't see their cow's hoof. They caste spells on unsuspecting men and make them fall in love with them and sometimes they kill them".

Gran looked knowingly at Ben and said, "so do you see

now Ben why you should't be flirting with Sarah".

Gran watched Ben and waited for him to speak. After some time, Ben got up and said "yeah Gran and I hear her dad is a Ligahoo, he made a deal with the devil so at night he changes into a werewolf so he can go around murdering little old ladies in their beds, without getting caught". Ben looked at Gran and held her gaze "so you better watch out Gran" he said.

After that Ben and Granny's relationship became more strained. Gran seemed to snipe at Ben every time she could and especially at the end of term when our test results came out. At the end of each school year we all did tests in all our different subjects, then the teachers would add up all the marks to work out our overall percentages. I was always ranked one of the top five pupils in my class out of a total of forty children. The only time I got any real attention from Gran was when she scrutinised my school reports. After reading my report she would pat me on the head and say "smart girl, your father would be proud".

Toby was always ranked about fifteenth out of forty children and after studying his report - she would also pat Toby on the head and tell him he could do better.

Ben on the other hand who was forever bunking off school was always ranked one of the five children at the bottom of his class. Gran on reading Ben's reports always seemed to take a great offence at this, as though his low ranking was a personal shame on her. I despaired at Ben most of the time as he was always pranking about and bunking off school and he never attended church anymore, but I always felt a bit sorry for him, when Gran laid into him with her sharp tongue, every time she got his school report.

One time Gran read Ben's report and he'd come in fortieth place out of forty children in his class. Gran screamed Ben's name at the top of her lungs and Ben stood in front of her visibly shaking. Gran got her big hard hand and wacked Ben with all her might around his head. Ben's eyes brimmed full but he tried to fight back the tears.

Gran shouted at the top of her voice "boy you are a complete and total dunce! You are dunce, dunce, dunce! You come fortieth out of forty children - Oh God have mercy upon me - the shame of it - you came last, last I say, every single child in your class is cleverer than you!" Gran continued "your father would be turning in his grave".

By this stage the tears began to flow freely down Ben's face.

Gran continued "Jesus Christ you are a disgrace, you make me shamed to call you my grandson".

At this Ben ran upstairs trying to disguise his sobbing.

I felt winded by the cruelty of Gran's words.

When Gran went into the kitchen, Toby looked up at me with big sad eyes, he sighed quietly. "Poor Ben".
I stroked Toby's head. "Yeah" I sighed back.

"But I don't understand Connie" Toby paused and then continued "how can Gran be so evil when she's supposed to be so religious?!"

Chapter 6

After that incident something in me changed, not only did I now view Gran as an evil old witch, I also became quite inwardly reflective. Before that I had gone through life seeing it as a series of random events. But now I saw the joined-up dots of my sad and unlucky life. I thought about Daddy dying a slow and agonising death, and Mummy turning from a beautiful elegant woman to a pathetic drunk and us three children being banished to the back end of Trinidad to an evil old hag disguised as our Gran. I went to church and prayed for a miracle, for an end to to the drudgery of our lives; I lit candles in church and went to confession. I read the bible looking for inspiration to effect change, but nothing changed.

One day at school my friend Martha turned to me and said "what's wrong with you these days Connie, it's as though someone knocked all the stuffing out of you and you are just a walking shadow".

I tried to brush it off by quoting Shakespeare and said "yes a walking shadow".

"Out, out, brief candle! Life's but a walking shadow, a poor player that struts and frets his hour upon the stage and is heard no more. It is a tale told by an idiot, full of sound and fury, signifying nothing".

Martha looked at me, I expected her to laugh, to congratulate me on remembering the Scottish play so well, but she looked at me square in the eyes and put her hand on my shoulder. "Don't do that Connie" she said "stop acting clever when you feel so sad".

She had caught me out, caught me off guard, her big brown, kind eyes and her sympathetic voice, tugged at my heart strings and without any control over my emotions, I collapsed into a heap, tears falling freely for what seemed like an age. I became aware that children were crowding around me in the playground; it was unusual to see older kids cry. Martha shouted at them and shooed them away and guided me to a secluded part of the playground.

Martha coaxed me to reveal what I was feeling. I was usually a private person but something about Martha was so soothing that I began to unravel what seemed to me the tragedy that was my life thus far. Through tearful sobs I told her about Dad and Mum and Gran and the silent regime at home, the overload of religion being pushed down our throats and the evil tongue that Gran dished out especially to Ben.

Martha listened quietly until I had finished my tale of woe. Then she looked down and took my hand, she held it and said thoughtfully "I want you to share all your troubles with me from now on Connie, don't bottle it up again, it's not good for you. A problem shared is a problem halved. My Mum says, if your store up all your troubles in your head and don't let them out, your head can't cope and all the thoughts get jumbled up and you end up, with a sickness of the mind that can't be cured. My Uncle Krish has a sickness of the mind, my Mum said he stored all his troubles in his brain and never let them out and his poor brain just couldn't cope anymore and all his thoughts exploded all at once, and now his thoughts are all jumbled up and he walks around talking to himself. Now he lives like a vagrant in the grounds of the College of the Immaculate Conception in town. The priests take pity on him and make sure he has food, while he meditates and rocks back and forwards and speaks to himself... Will you promise me Connie that you won't get yourself in this state again, don't you feel lighter for having shared your problems with me?"

Suddenly I realised I did feel lighter, like a weight had been lifted away from my chest. The knots in my stomach had loosened and my cares seemed less burdensome.

After that Martha and I talked and talked, about school work, about the meaning of life and about things that were troubling us. We talked about Shakespeare and world peace and the ozone layer. We challenged each other to glean more and more knowledge from anywhere and everywhere. We became bosom buddies inseparable in all things and she often invited me to her house after school for dinner. Surprisingly Gran did not object because Martha's uncle was the parish priest. Occasionally Gran even let me stay overnight and life became for me bearable again.

One-day Martha said as we told each other everything, that she had a confession to make. I was intrigued. "What is it?" I gasped expectantly.

"Promise you won't get upset with me" she said.

"I promise" I said without thinking.

"I really fancy your brother Ben" she blurted out "he's so good looking and stylish, he seems so carefree. I dream about him and think about him all the time. I know it's not logical but I think I'm in love with him!"

"Oh my God" I gasped. "Martha, the boy is only sixteen and we are seventeen - do you want to be a cradle snatcher?! And anyway he's already seeing Sarah".

"What Sweet shop Sarah?" Martha huffed.

"Yeah, that's the one, so you know her?" I asked.

"Yes, I do" Martha sighed "and he will soon dump her when he sees her cow foot! People says she's a female devil, that's why she is so beautiful. No one could be that beautiful naturally. Have you seen her, wow she looks good enough to eat".

"Yes" I agreed "that's what Ben says. He says she's sweeter than all the sweets in her parent's sweet shop".

"Oh boy" whispered Martha "how do I compete with that".

A few months later Martha and I were discussing the emancipation of slaves that we'd learnt in history, when Martha said wistfully "wouldn't it be good if we could emancipate ourselves from this back-end hole of a village and free ourselves of these shackles that bind us here".

She then formed her fingers into imaginary scissors and began snipping around us both "snip, snip, snip" she was saying "snip, snip, snip". She looked so serious and so comical at the same time with her imaginary scissors that I burst out laughing. "Girl" I exclaimed "what are you doing?"

"Can't you see?" Martha said seriously "I'm freeing us both from this imperfect life, from now on we are going to study hard and make something of ourselves, we are going to rise up from here and create a perfect life for ourselves". She paused and then smiled and hugged me tight "promise me Connie Costello that you will create a perfect life for yourself, you will not deviate from this plan until your wish becomes reality".

"I promise" I said eagerly and meant it.

Martha then stood up she saluted me and said "and I Martha Grainger promise you Connie Costello that I will create a perfect life for myself, and I will not deviate from this plan until my wish becomes reality so help me God".

"Amen" I shouted and saluted back.

Chapter 7

Ben felt that his bond with Gran as fickle as it was, had now been broken irretrievably as he put it. He didn't see any point in trying to please Gran anymore and quite to the contrary his every action now seemed in open defiance of her.

Ben had now taken to running off each day after school to meet Sarah. He said that he and Sarah were soul mates; he said she had in his view, a superior intelligence and that he could learn more from her, than any of the teachers at school. He said she could convey in simplified terms the most complex of issues. It was clear to me that Ben was in love.

So it was left to me to walk home with Toby each day. On such a day we were walking home, it was the rainy season so the air was thick and humid. The atmosphere was pregnant with moisture and I could feel my hair beginning to frizz, which annoyed me. Toby was chattering aimlessly and I lost in my own thoughts, feigned interest in his small boy chatter.

I looked up and I could see only wisps of blue sky through the clouds but it was still fairly bright. Then rapidly the sky turned overcast and a cool breeze began to surround us. Toby looked up and exclaimed "Oh God the Cobo's are coming for us". I looked up and saw about a dozen or so Corbeaux. They were circling the sky... their black bodies permeating a sinister darkness above us.

Toby's eyes widened he seemed paralysed by fear, he gasped "Gran says the black vultures are the devil incarnate". As I looked up at black bodies swirling above us, Toby's words gripped me and my breath caught in my throat.

After catching my breath, seized by both fear and a desire to seem unafraid, I shouted at Toby "well don't look up then" and I grabbed his arm and began marching forward with deliberate large strides. As we walked I could feel the sky darken another hue and small fat droplets began to fall on our heads.

Toby continued his voice faltering "Gran says the Cobo's are dirty scavengers, when you see them, you know death, and disease are near, Gran says Cobo's feed on dead flesh and are the most disgusting birds of the sky".

At this point I heard one of the black vultures squawk a piercing scream and a cold shiver travelled slowly down my spine. The air was cold and I was becoming uneasy. To hide my cowardice, I said to Toby in a harsh tone "shut up and stop talking rubbish. My teacher who knows much more than Gran says vultures are the most useful birds because they clean up the environment. When an animal dies, usually it is left to rot and stink which causes rats, but we are lucky in Trinidad because here we have these Corbeaux crows that feed on the dead animals and clean up the streets".

Just as I finished my little speech, a large black Corbeau flew down and landed in front of us. I was alarmed at how large it was close up and I was concerned at its proximity to us.

He cawed a raspy eerie cry and his large sharp eyes, which were red rimmed, held us both in an intense gaze. Rhythmically it spread its large glossy black wings, revealing white tips. The wings were so large when outstretched that it blocked our path. I had never been this near to a Corbeau before and I was transfixed by the horrendous beauty of it. It was paradoxically both majestic and extremely ugly. I noticed its droopy iron-grey cowl covering his neck, like a scarf. My fear increased when he moved closer to us on his long gawky legs and I gripped Toby's hand tighter. Slowly the bird opened his beak and looked as though he were going to start pecking at us, Toby and I screamed and backed away, and then the bird, squawked again and flew away.

As he flew we saw the other Corbeaux follow him into the sky, squawking and flapping their wings. We watched them until they were tiny black dots in the distance. Suddenly the clouds seemed to disappear and it was bright and sunny again.

We continued to walk home in horrified silence, neither one of us able to really identify what had just happened.

As we walked I tried to formulate some words in my head that might reassure Toby. I was thinking about saying that nothing had happened, except a large bird flew down and landed near to us, it was nothing out the ordinary really. I had almost convinced myself of the normalcy of what had occurred and I was about to voice my carefully constructed reassurance to Toby, when Toby turned to me with watery eyes.

"I just remembered" Toby blurted, his eyes widened "Gran said Cobo's eat the flesh of the dead because it helps them communicate with the other side".

My blood ran cold from my head, down to the base of my spine.

Chapter 8

One sunny afternoon, Toby and I walked home bathed in golden sunshine without a care in the world. The sun was low in the cloudless sky. Toby alternated between skipping around and dribbling his ball. I dreamily meandered behind him. When we got home Ben was already there and he quickly slipped me a note which simply said "she's in monster granny mood". I discretely passed the note to Toby.

Gran stomped about the house banging doors and slamming dishes, the three of us silently did our chores and homework, trying to keep out of her way. She seemed in a particularly bad mood.

After dinner she sat us down and told us that our cousin Shanti was getting married. She said that the baby was due in a few months and Shanti and her fiancé, now wanted to get married to ensure that the baby would be born as a child of wedlock.

Gran was clearly irritated, she raised her voice when she said that the wedding was in a couple of months and we were all invited to it. Gran said she did not care that the baby would be born in wedlock; she felt that Shanti had committed a sin by getting pregnant out of wedlock, in the first place. Gran said she could not condone the flagrant breach of God's laws. In her view the child would never be legitimate. She ranted and raved that she would not be a hypocrite, she would not attend the wedding on principle!

She continued preaching to us about breaking God's laws, about how the world was now too willing to condone heathen behaviour, she went on and on shouting and preaching until my ears felt saturated, my head hurt and I began to switch off.

But suddenly my ears pricked up when she said, "I am putting my foot down! Toby is too young to be exposed to this promiscuous wedding!"

Toby looked down at his fingers, he wasn't good at hiding his feelings he looked forlorn and disappointed.

Ben and I looked at each other expectant.

Gran continued "But you two is big people now, if you want to go, please yourself!"

Ben winked at me and I secretly smiled inside.

After a few days of building up courage, Ben and I told Gran that we wanted to go to the wedding. Gran was not pleased, but to her credit she agreed to give us both an allowance for new clothes and to buy a present.

The weeks that followed were happy ones; all I could think of was the wedding. I chatted endlessly with Martha about what I'd wear, where to buy my outfit, how to do my hair and makeup, what present to buy for the happy couple. After school Martha and I went to the shops to browse at dresses and to buy fashion magazines, so we could get ideas for makeup and hairstyles. I was lucky that the sales were on and I eventually found a floaty pale peach dress, which held me in all the right places and really showed off my slim but shapely figure. When Martha saw me in it she said "well girl you look hot".

Toby was disappointed not to be going to the wedding and Ben and I despite our excitement felt sorry for him. We could read Toby like an open book and he was suffering. It was so obvious that even Gran picked up on Toby's unhappiness.

A week before the wedding Gran said "cheer up Toby I

have a big surprise for you". Toby's reaction at the mention of a surprise was measured, but we could see that he did perk up.

One Saturday Gran went out early and when she came home she brought home a little puppy. It was mainly white with short fur, short legs and a black patch on one eye. Gran said it was a terrier, as she proudly presented it to Toby.

Toby's brown eyes widened, he looked visibly surprised. Tentatively he checked "Gran is this dog for me to keep?!" Gran grinned so wide that her features softened and she said, "yes Toby it's your dog, but you have to look after it mind".

Toby did a little jig and squealed with delight, he placed it on his lap and hugged it. The dog looked up at Toby and licked his ears. Toby raised his head "thanks Gran" he smiled "I love it, I'm going to call it Bandit because it has a black patch on one eye".

I looked at Gran and she seemed really pleased and unexpectedly I was awash with a pang of love for her.

Toby's time was occupied after that, he and his friend Ramone as well as Ramone's dad made a lead for the dog, a house for the dog, bathed him, fed him and took him out for walks and runs. Ben and I were relieved that we could now concentrate on the wedding without feeling guilty about leaving Toby behind.

Chapter 9

The day of the wedding I told Gran that I would get ready at Martha's house as I didn't want Gran to see me all dressed up, in case she made me change or rub off makeup or anything else she disapproved off. I arrived at Martha's house early, so she could take her time doing my hair and makeup. She washed and blow dried my hair, rolled it in large curls and then lightly brushed it out.

She spent a long time doing my eyes with pastel eye shadow, black mascara and eye liner; she finished off with a deep burgundy lipstick and a touch of blusher on my cheeks. When I slipped on my dress and shoes and looked in the mirror I could hardly recognise myself, I looked really pretty.

As Ben was getting ready at home, I had arranged to meet him at the bus stop. As I happily approached the bus stop, my heart skipped a beat when I noticed that Ben was not alone and I was shocked to see that Sarah was with him, arms intertwined. As I approached, Ben eyed me expectantly but said nonchalantly "I decided to bring Sarah as my plus one".

"What plus one?" I blurted "who said anything about plus ones".

Ben looked at Sarah and smiled, Sarah looked embarrassed, Ben said "relax Connie, I called Shanti and asked her and she said it was fine".

As the bus pulled up and we got on, Ben turned to me and said "by the way you look nice!"

I felt really upset - how dare he bring Sarah leaving me to be a gooseberry. If he had told me in advance maybe I could have brought Martha. But this was typical Ben, always thinking of just himself.

Ben and Sarah sat together and I sat behind them nursing my bad mood. I imagined myself on my own at the wedding, not knowing many people and all the weeks of preparation now seemed pointless, I felt like crying.

I observed them from a distance; they were so annoying, they really got on well together. Sarah was a natural beauty with her golden-brown hair and green eyes, she looked like a model. She was tall almost Ben's height. She was wearing a long frilly cream dress with a low neckline, she was so delicate and feminine. Ben complemented her, in his grey pinstripe suit and sharp white shirt, they looked like a couple straight out of the glossy magazines, that Martha and I had bought to get ideas.

Looking at them I felt a pang of jealousy, with all my hairdo, make up and fancy dress, with matching shoes and handbag, there was no doubt about it, Sarah was much prettier than me. I felt a sinking hollow feeling in my stomach.

As soon as we got off the bus, we could hear the tassa band playing from a distance. Ben holding Sarah's hand explained to her that tassa drum bands are associated with Indian weddings. He projected his voice in a very showy way and told her that the band consisted of several large bass drums, usually made from mango tree trunks. He continued as though giving a speech, the drums make a deep sound and there is usually someone in the band that plays the brass cymbals. He smiled at her and said playfully, "and did you know tassa drums are played with sticks made from wild sugar cane".

Sarah gripped his hand tighter and swung it in the air;

she laughed "you are so knowledgeable, Ben".

Ben smiled smugly.

I looked away and thought of Gran calling Ben a dunce, inwardly I chuckled.

The wedding was loud and busy. Shanti wore a red sari and then changed into a yellow sari and then lastly changed into her white wedding dress. She was heavily pregnant but pregnancy clearly agreed with her and her skinny flat chested body had nicely filled out. Shanti was not one of life's beauties but she looked good and her husband was actually really good looking.

As soon as the ceremonies were over, Ben told me he was going to find Mum. Apparently, she was in the bar area and he wanted to introduce Sarah to her, he asked me if I wanted to go with them, but I didn't feel ready to see Mum just yet as I had not seen her for some while.

As Sarah and Ben left me sitting on my own, my resentment towards them returned, now I was truly a sad little gooseberry. I looked around at all the young girls heavily made up and decked with jewellery and I was astounded at how grown up they were trying to be, but I had to admit and admire that some of them could walk competently in very high heels. As I looked around bored I suddenly I met Shanti's eye and she ran over to me, I stood up and she hugged me. "Look at you all grown up" she smiled.

"You look blooming" I replied looking at her round tummy.

Shanti sighed "girl I am so happy, I met Charles a while ago, I always fancied him from way back, but I knew deep down he was out of my league. But you know me; I pursued him until he gave in and went on a date with me. Well girl", she gushed, "I didn't play hard to get and we slept together on the first date and bam I got pregnant straight away". She laughed and continued, "I knew he didn't really like me that much but his parents said he had to make an honest woman out of me as I was carrying his child. He reluctantly agreed but I knew he wasn't really happy. But luck was on my side Connie and as the months went on and we spent more time together, he says he's grown to love me and his little baby I'm carrying and now we are like any other regular couple, in love, married and having a baby..." she gasped... "I'm so happy Connie, it's everything I could wish for. His parents are well off, they have given us a small starter house which they have completely furnished and we are going to move in after our little honeymoon to Barbados".

I looked at Shanti - she was radiant, her happiness was palpable, but before I could respond, someone grabbed her hand and whisked her away. She waved and blew me a kiss as she went.

I sat down, patently aware I was on my own again, I watched some loved up couples in the middle of the dance floor and on the edge I noticed Sarah and Ben cuddling tight and kissing each other, I looked away suddenly embarrassed.

As I looked away, I heard a voice close behind me saying "did you bang your head". I turned around and saw a young man about my age looking at me and he said again "did you bang your head".

I stood up to look at him straight in the eye and said "are you speaking to me?"

"Yes darling" he smiled revealing slightly crooked teeth "I was wondering if you hurt your head when you fell out of heaven!"

I looked at him incredulous, he was about my height, he smelled like he'd put on the whole bottle of after shave and his gelled hair was slicked back in a low quiff. He was slim and was handsome, in a pretty boy kind of way.

I laughed. "Are you single?".

"Well I'm glad you asked, yes I am single" he answered smiling.

"Yes, well I'm not surprised" I said curtly "do you really think those cheesy one liners, give you real pulling power with the girls!"

His smile slipped, he opened his mouth to respond but he seemed lost for words. I realised just in time that I had offended him, so I quickly extended my hand to him and gave him my best smile, I said "Hi, my name is Connie, let's work on your chat up lines".

His smile quickly reappeared and he said "OK, then let's do that and by the way my name is Preston".

Chapter 10

Preston turned out to be intelligent, he was doing his A-levels like me and we had a lot in common. We chatted easily until Shanti and Ruby came to grab me to dance. I pulled Preston's hand so he came with us to the dance floor. To say he couldn't dance was an understatement. His dance moves were a little jerky and uncoordinated and he waved his arms about with too much enthusiasm, but he was attentive towards me and made sure he went to the bar to get me drinks, as soon as my glass was empty.

Later into the night though, I noticed his attention towards me was becoming distracted and I was disconcerted to notice that he kept on taking furtive glances towards Ruby. Ruby was as glamourous as ever; her long hair was curled at the ends. Her make-up was flawless and her signature red lipstick made the most of her bowtie shaped lips. She was still extremely attractive. She was wearing a silver figure hugging short dress, which emphasised her oversized bosom and shapely backside. Her four-inch silver heels highlighted her long and well-formed legs. Ruby was dancing provocatively, her hips swayed rhythmically, I reluctantly admired the way her body was completely in tune with the music. Preston tried to keep attentive towards me, but eventually as though mesmerised by Ruby, he became totally focussed on her. I felt my heart sink to my stomach for the second time that day.

Eventually Preston asked Ruby to dance to a slow tune and as their bodies locked together in dance, I looked away, it was too hurtful to watch and walked back to where I was sitting earlier. From my vantage point I watched the couples on the dance floor, Sarah and Ben, Shanti and her new husband and several others including Preston and Ruby. I felt deflated, like I had been kicked in the stomach.

I sat like that for what seemed an age, I was bored and lonely and decided it was time to seek out Mum. As I turned to get up, my eyes were distracted by a pair of bulging biceps. I followed the arms to the face and found him looking at me. He smiled at me and I felt a flush of embarrassment wash over me. His name was Michael he was a mechanic, he wasn't formerly educated but he was very knowledgeable. He was lovely, a real hunk of a man solid and taut and tall. He had rugged intriguing features and I was flattered that he wanted to speak to me.

He was easy to speak to and asked me a lot about myself, my thoughts and feelings, my plans. Conversation flowed, spanning our lives and histories. I felt like I had known him all my life, invisible strings seemed to tie us together. He complimented me and said I was pretty. I felt like the only girl in the room. My insecurities about Sarah and Ruby melted away into nothingness.

We chatted for ages and then he said "Connie would you do me the honour of dancing with me?" I thought my heart would explode with happiness. We danced cheek to cheek for the rest of the night. At the end, we were dancing to *Chris de Burgh - Lady in Red*, and as he sang the words into my ear, I melted into a state of pure bliss.

At the end of the night we had already made plans to meet again.

On the way home on the bus, Sarah and Ben were loved up, but I no longer felt any bitterness. Sarah fell asleep on Ben and I was lost in my own pure untainted joy.

Myself and Martha had read loads of Mills and Boon books, but I didn't really know anything about love, but instinctively I knew that I was in love. The sated feeling stayed with me every time I thought of Michael.

Ben's voice broke me from my reverie. "Connie was that Michael Moore you were dancing with for hours?"

"I don't know his surname" I stuttered "do you know him".

"Yes" Ben answered, "he runs a garage with his old man up on the hill, he's a good guy".

A warm feeling of bliss filled me, it was good to get Ben's approval. Ben continued "don't worry I won't tell Gran if you want to see him, it can be our secret".

I was grateful and happy all at once. "Oh, thanks Ben" I gushed.

Ben was chatty, I sensed alcohol had made him loquacious, he was wittering on and on about Shanti, Ruby, Kelvin and Harry, but I wasn't really listening, lost in my own thoughts of Michael.

Then Ben laughed "didn't Mum look well, I don't think she's drinking as much".

A panic stabbed me in my heart, *oh God forgive me*, I thought to myself, I hadn't even gone to see or speak to my own mother!

Chapter 11

I told Martha in detail about the wedding and I had intended to tell her all about Michael but when it came to it, I found myself omitting any reference to Michael. For some reason, I realised I wanted to keep Michael all to myself, a protected part of me, I didn't want to share him with anyone.

My relationship with Michael swept me off my feet and before I knew it we were a couple. He was gentle and kind to me and made my first intimate encounter amazing. It felt so right, so natural, his smell, his taste, his lips. His delicate stroking made my nerve receptors come alive, in tingling electric convulsions. We attacked each other with a trust and rhythm of pure chemistry, as he whispered to me "don't worry, Connie, I won't hurt you". His hot swollen flesh felt innocent and warm as he drove himself deeper and deeper. My body responded and rippled like the waves of the ocean. After we lay side by side, breathless and spent. We gazed at each other in awe. Lost for words we held each other tight, gentle and tender. In the distance, a clap of thunder jolted us back to the present and we listened with soft breaths, to the patter of sweet rain. We fell asleep in each other's arms.

I only felt happy and whole when I was with him, I missed him when I was away from him. I carried on studying with Martha but I made excuses to leave her and spend time with Michael by saying I was spending time with my cousins Shanti and Ruby. Ben proved a real ally and with his help I convinced Gran that I was studying or staying over at Martha's, when I was with Michael.

Michael was an only child and he lived in a separate self-contained dwelling annexed to his parents' house, which was on the same site as the garage which he and his father ran together. It turned out that there was a four-year age gap between us, I was nineteen and he was twenty-three. It felt good having an older boyfriend because he was very sure of himself, so I let him take the lead in all things. He also had money so our social life was good and we went out frequently to clubs, the cinema, restaurants and often to the beach.

Pleasure welled up inside of me every time I thought of him and for the first time since Daddy had died I felt good, my studies were going well, life with Gran was more bearable, I had a gorgeous boyfriend whom I loved to pieces and who loved me and to top it off, Mum had started to visit us at Grans from time to time.

One day, about six months into our relationship, we were sitting on Michael's bed and he was twirling my hair in his hands, when he said nonchalantly "Connie Costello would you ever consider marrying me?"

I was initially elated but I was taken aback by the way he posed his question and the way doubt had crept into his voice.

"Michael Moore" I answered "of course I would consider marrying you, but why would you doubt me in that way?"

Michael grinned in his boyish way, endearing him to my heart, he looked embarrassed and paused as though lost for words.

"Come on Michael" I urged trying to keep the slight panic out of my voice "tell me!"

Michael was clearly struggling to find words, he looked thoughtfully at his hands and then said still looking down "well Connie let's face it you are a big-time college girl, you are going places, you have plans to go University".

"And?" I asked.

"And" he continued his eyes now fixed on me, "I'm a small-town motor mechanic, do you really think you could settle for me long term?"

I was hurt, really hurt and before I could control it tears welled up in my eyes, threatening to spill over.

"Michael, I love you with all my heart" I said, "why would you think me so shallow?"

Michael enveloped me in his strong arms "I'm sorry" he whispered in my ear and he kissed the top of my head.

That conversation seemed to be a catalyst. After that Michael and I began to make plans for our future. We decided that we could get married in a year or two and that he could support me during my degree at University.

We agreed to tell Gran about us after my twenty-first birthday. His parents already knew all about me.

One grey and overcast day, my mood matched the weather, I brooded about Daddy and his painful death and Mum and her drinking. Melancholy welled up in me. Before I reached Michael's place, I saw him running towards me, a vision of happy good health and youth. He hugged me toward him and grinned. His boyish good looks and his pure unadulterated joy, charmed me to my core. My sadness dissipated. He beamed "Connie I've got something for you". Inside his annex I looked around, my mind's eye immediately imagined flowers or a boxed present tied with a bow. I scanned the room quickly but I could not see anything. He approached his bedside table and opened the drawer, my heart skipped a beat and I felt giddy, *Oh God,* I thought to myself, he's bought me a ring!

He approached me looking shy and coy. I looked at his hands and in them he held a piece of paper. I was blown away, my heart was going to burst with happiness, before thinking I blurted out laughing "Michael did you get a marriage licence for us?"

Michael looked down confused at the piece of paper in his hand. "No Connie" he answered in a deflated voice "I wrote you a poem".

I painted a bright smile on my face and answered with false enthusiasm "oh how lovely - let's hear it then" as my heart sank to the floor.

Michael looked at me long and hard, after a long pause he answered "okay".

He opened the paper in his hands cleared his throat and began to sing.

"Connie Costello,

You're the one for me,

I want you for my breakfast,

I want you for my tea.

Connie Costello,

I thank the Lord above,

For sending me,

My one true love"

I looked at Michael he was a true gentleman, I loved him

with every fibre of my being. He hadn't bought me a present wrapped in a box or a diamond ring, but what he gave me was priceless, it was his unconditional love. I pulled him to me and kissed him deep and slow. My chest puffed out and swelled. Joy and happiness flowed through my veins like nectar.

Chapter 12

The long summer vacation had started and us three children being at home all the time seemed to irritate Gran. After several altercations with Gran we all tried to keep out of her way. Toby spent a lot of time at Ramone's house and Ben spent most of his time with Sarah. I spent all my time with Michael, as Martha had gone on holiday with her parents.

A few weeks into the holidays, Michael and his father got a big job on with a taxi firm and Michael was too busy to spend much time with me. I was bored so I decided to go to visit Shanti and her new baby Crystal.

On the bus there, I noticed that the sky was cloudless and a blinding hue of blue, the sun shone unnaturally brightly through the windows. I was bathed in a bright bubble and I felt dizzy and faint. I thought of Gran and her unpleasant ways and I longed for our cushioned life before Daddy had died. My thoughts wandered aimlessly until it turned to our landlord Sam Ramlochan and I recalled that he'd promised to "fix Daddy good and proper" and I wondered whether he had in fact put a curse on him. Dad was gone and Mum was as good as gone now and I felt that effectively the three of us siblings were now orphans, caste out at sea drifting all alone. I felt empty in the pit of my stomach. As much as I tried, I felt no love or any real affection towards Gran.

As I got off the bus I tripped and almost fell off. The scorching sun seemed to burn the top of my head, the light was too bright and I felt blinded.

When I got to Shanti's she was excessively happy and enthusiastic. She reminded me of a bumble bee buzzing around in her brightly coloured yellow dress. She said she was so happy, as she showed me around her new home. It was bright, airy and sparsely furnished but the furniture that was there was of an excellent quality. The baby's room was filled with toys, furniture, and a frilly crib. The baby was smooth, fat and light skinned, she slept peacefully in her little wicker basket. As we left the baby sleeping, she told me her husband was at work and they were saving up for another holiday. She said that their honeymoon was fabulous. Shanti giggled "girl I even tried a blue cocktail, called a blue lagoon and it made me really silly and I got brave and even did Karaoke, it was so fun". She continued "my life is practically perfect Connie". Albeit I was pleased for Shanti - her good fortune and her happiness which I could tell were genuine, were getting on my nerves and my head hurt.

Just then I heard Ruby's voice at the door, she breezed in with a large fluffy white teddy bear. "this is for Baby Crystal" she announced with her pouty lip glossed lips. God, Ruby got on my nerves too, why did she always look so damn good. She was wearing skinny jeans and a tight-fitting crop top.

I suddenly realised that I had come to visit without bringing a present for the baby and shame stung at my face creating a burning sensation.

Ruby looked at me her head tilted and exclaimed "Hi Connie what's wrong with you, you look like shit" she paused and sighed dramatically "shall I make us all some coffee?"

My head hurt, I couldn't think of a witty response fast enough, so I let her comment go unanswered. She made the coffee and soon we were gossiping and catching up just like old times. I began to relax, losing myself in the sumptuous leather sofa.

It turned out that Ruby and Preston were now officially an item, Ruby had got a job as an exotic dancer at an exclusive club in Town and was getting paid loads to dance around a metal pole. Shanti and I couldn't understand the need for the metal pole but we were fascinated. She said she was going to support Preston through university. Preston had also got a driving job at weekends, which would supplement their income. They planned to get married as soon as Preston got his degree. Ruby said her Mum and Dad adored Preston, they were impressed that she had ended up with a College boy with good prospects. Ruby told us all about the many boyfriends she had had before but that Preston was different as he was a virgin when she met him. At that Shanti giggled uncontrollably and asked for details, which Ruby readily supplied in her crude way. As usual Shanti lapped up everything detail Ruby described.

I desperately wanted to share my own experiences and was resentful that I could not share my news. I contemplated telling them about Michael and our plans. But I knew I couldn't trust them not to talk about me to everyone and I couldn't guarantee that Gran wouldn't find out about it on the grapevine and kick me out on the street. The risk of telling them was too great. As Dad used to say, "loose lips sinks ships". I consoled myself that a year from now, I would tell them all about my plans and it would be my wedding we'd be discussing.

As I sat there contentedly, I sipped the coffee that had now started to get cold, it was bitter, it tasted rancid and I couldn't help but to gag. It tasted off. Ruby and Shanti stared at me shocked, as I spat the coffee back into the cup. "Has the milk gone off" I spluttered. Ruby gazed at me, cocked her head and laughed "I already finished my coffee long ago and it was fine". Shanti sipped her coffee "mine is good too" she added.

I started to feel unwell, I felt a bile taste snake its way from my stomach to my throat and before I knew it I was throwing up all over Shanti's new plush leather sofa. Shanti jumped up and screamed "get up! get up! yuh ruining the sofa, yuh stupid fool!"

Ruby looked on incredulous and then she burst out laughing, big loud deep belly laughs. Shanti ran to the sink and grabbed a wet cloth, I watched helpless as she cleaned up the nasty looking vomit which was now sinking into the leather creases.

Shanti looked at me exasperated, she shouted "go and clean up yourself you damn arse!"

Ruby guffawed again and laughed her fitful deep belly laugh over and over again.

In the bathroom, I felt so embarrassed, I wished I could leave before I had to face them again. I cleaned myself up as best as I could and came out of the bathroom smoothing my dress.

Ruby looked up narrowing her eyes and said stifling a giggle "are you alright Connie dear? I told you, you look like shit"

Shanti looked at me her face softening "sorry I shouted at you", she apologised. "Don't worry you didn't stain the leather, it cleaned up good, I was just worried because it's a brand new sofa! Maybe you should go home now if you don't feel well".

"Yes" I answered softly. I grabbed my handbag without looking at Ruby who was still giggling and walked to the door. Shanti walked me to the porch. She smiled at me.

"Thanks for visiting Connie, I hope you don't mind if I don't kiss you, in case what you have is contagious".

"No, that's ok" I replied embarrassed "I'm so sorry Shanti".

Shanti put her hand on my arm and smiled. "Don't worry Connie, no harm done, I was just remembering how I thought coffee tasted rancid when I first got pregnant".

Out of nowhere, Ruby appeared from inside, her hands on her waist. "Well clearly that's not Connie's problem, her being a proper Catholic virgin girl an' all" she laughed maliciously.

Before I could answer she turned and walked back inside the house.

Chapter 13

On the bus back, I found myself nursing my hatred of Ruby. I wished her fat and ugly, I wished her horrible injuries with that stupid metal pole she had to dance with. A couple of mosquitoes buzzed around my ears and nibbled at my ankles making me more irritable.

As I slowly walked home, the sun was still unbearably hot, I felt drained and flattened by the heat. As I approached the house, confusion scrambled my thoughts at the scene before me.

They were all in the yard, Gran's mouth was open, a loud long scream piercing the air around. Toby was crying long tears pouring from his eyes and snot running from his nose. A small figure was hanging from the first landing of the outdoor steps. As I got closer I could see the figure hanging was Bandit the dog, his lead was strangling his neck, his head was bent at a lopsided angle. His eyes stared out at me glazed and bulging. His mouth hung open spittle dribbling down and his tongue drooped out thickened and pink.

Just then Mr Sookoo ran out from next door "hold up de dog" he shouted and rushed to support the weight of Bandit. At the side of my vision I saw Ben run down the stairs, a big scissors in his hand, I watched in slow motion as he cut the lead around Bandit's neck.

"Doh worry, Toby" Mr Sookoo said kindly "de dog still warm".

"Sing *Staying Alive*" Ben shouted to Toby. It seemed comical watching as Ben gave Bandit the kiss of life and pumped Bandit's chest, to the tune of Toby singing *Staying Alive* by the Bee Gees.

Bandit lay splayed on the ground all four limbs looking limp. His body pumped up and down by Ben, while his doggy eyes bulged out glazed and lifeless.

Overhead there is the deep raspy caw of a raven, I look up to see it's ebony wings in majestic flight.

"Ah, ah, ah, ah, staying alive, staying alive" Toby sings tunelessly, while my head spun all around, my vision blurred and I fell, the hard-concrete yard meeting my face.

When I woke I was on a chair on the porch. Gran was rocking on her rocking chair dabbing her eyes with a tissue. Mr Sookoo was kneeling near me with the smelling salts in his hand. "You fainted" he said patting my hand "let me make you all a pot of tea".

Gran looked at me "you alright?" she said. But before I could answer she sniffed "de dog dead you know... Ben digging a hole for him".

The dog was laid to rest and Toby gave it the rite of Extreme Unction, which gives the dead soul the strength to travel to the hereafter. Ramone's dad made a little wooden cross to mark the grave.

The next few days I was weak and threw up often. Gran said the shock was too much for me. Laying on my bed one day, Toby came in, his eyes still red rimmed from crying. He sat on the end of the bed looking forlorn. "Connie", he said in a small voice "do you think dogs have souls?"

"I think they do" I answered "all living things have souls".

"Do you think Bandit has gone to dog heaven or the regular heaven we all go to?" Toby questioned.

"I think" I said thoughtfully "all good souls go to

paradise, a beautiful universe, where life is always good and warm and kind. No one there gets old, gets hurt or dies. In paradise, every man, woman, child and animal lives in eternal happiness in the garden of Eden".

Toby smiled "I can imagine Bandit running around free without a lead in that beautiful garden". He paused and sighed "do you know it was my fault why he died, because I made his lead too long and he climbed up the stairs on his lead and then jumped and that's how he ended up hanging like that".

"It wasn't your fault Toby", I offered "sometimes sad things just happen".

Toby stood up "Gran said she'd get me a new dog, but I'm not sure I want another dog, I loved Bandit".

Gran came in the room just then, she said she was worried about me and that she had made an appointment with the doctor. She told me to get dressed straight away.

I was concerned to find Gran ready and waiting for me when I came downstairs, "Come on let's go" Gran said grabbing her handbag.

"Gran, you don't have to go with me" I said, "I'm twenty years old".

"I'm not having you fainting alone on the streets" Gran said harshly and I knew from her tone that further protest would be pointless.

At the doctor's office when the receptionist called my name, Gran got up to come in with me, I was mortified "Gran, they won't let you come in with me" I protested.

"Shut up" Gran barked "all my life I come to this doctor they won't turn me away". And in she walked with me.

As we sat down Gran began describing my symptoms I

fainted after a shock, she described what happened to Bandit, she told him I was vomiting and that I felt dizzy and faint.

The doctor examined me and asked me what I had eaten in the last few days. He then asked me if I might be pregnant.

At this Gran jumped up. "What kinda damn arse question is that doctor, this here is my granddaughter, she's a fine Catholic girl and a virgin, don't go insulting her and my family like that" she kissed her teeth and sat down.

The doctor looked at Gran and said in a sympathetic voice "I didn't mean to offend you both but it's a question I have to ask".

The doctor said the vomiting and dizziness were a result of gastroenteritis and prescribed some medicine. Gran seemed happy enough as we went to the chemist to pick up the medication. On the way home, she said "I knew it, you picked up something nasty from that promiscuous Shanti's house!"

Chapter 14

The vomiting continued but I hid it from Gran and pretended I was getting better. Michael and I had always been very careful, we practised the rhythm method of contraception, but Shanti's words had played on my mind.

Sick with worry I purchased a pregnancy kit as soon as I could and I was horrified when it indicated that I was indeed pregnant. My first thought was to tell Michael. I knew he would be pleased and would offer to marry me straight away. Thinking it through it seemed that everything would be ok.

But then I thought of telling Gran and how she would react to a Costello baby being conceived out of wedlock. I thought about how she had reacted when Shanti had got pregnant and I felt faint. I also thought of Martha and our perfect life plans. Having a baby so young would be an end to my medical career and University.

The next few days my thoughts and emotions swarmed all over the place going from one scenario to another, eventually enclosing me in an impenetrable world of torment.

On the day, I made up my mind to tell Michael, the exam results came out. I was elated, I had passed them all and got the grades to study medicine. But my happiness was punctuated with worry and uncertainty about being pregnant. In my confused state, I decided to tell Michael anyway and to discuss all options with him. Michael was my soul mate we would decide together.

When I got to Michael's his father advised me that he was on a breakdown recovery and would not be back for several hours. I was tired and fed up and needed a friend. I desperately needed to share this with someone, the burden of dealing with this on my own was beginning to wear me down. In the scorching hot sun, I decided hastily to reveal everything to Martha.

By the time I got to Martha's I was exhausted. Martha's mum greeted me warmly and congratulated me on my exam results. She said Martha had also done well and had got into University to do Media and Fashion. Martha's father had taken her out shopping to buy her a car, it was an early present for her twenty-first birthday and for passing her exams. Martha's mum said I was welcome to wait, but I declined her offer. I felt deflated, how could I burden Martha with my silly mistake on such a joyful day. I had messed up all our plans for a perfect life, well my plans at least.

The sun was now low in the sky and I didn't know where to turn, I walked about aimlessly until I came to a busy walled square, teeming with people waiting at a bus stop and taxi rank. I thought about getting a bus to Shanti's or to Mum's, but my confused thoughts converged into a migraine. The sun, the walled square, the people and the noise all seemed to spin and tilt and fearing I might fall, I quickly lowered myself to sit on the wall.

I sat with my head in my hands until the world stopped spinning, I think I fell asleep. I awoke it seemed to me several hours later, with an overwhelming sense of calm. The square was now quiet and hardly anyone was around. At the corner of my eye I sensed I was not alone and when I turned I saw that sitting next to me was a very old man. His skin seemed to be tanned the deepest shade of black, it was creased and corrugated, prune-like. On his head was a shock of very white hair. He smiled at me, a crooked half smile and his teeth beamed white against his very black skin. He held out his hand to me and I held it, he seemed to be radiating a still calm. "You are in trouble child" he said in a soothing voice "would you like your troubles to go away".

Silent tears formed at my eyes and I realised that I wanted more than anything for this pregnancy to go away. I let the tears flow unashamed and grateful for the relief the release of tears created.

He handed me a printed card it said **Ms C La Corbel- Clairvoyant and Midwifery Services**.

He smiled crookedly again – he pointed to a white house across the square "go there" he said, "she will help you".

I looked up at the house, it stood out in the gleaming sun its white facade proud and tall in the landscape. "How did you know I was in trouble" I said confused. He didn't answer. I turned to look at him, but he was gone, not a trace of him left behind except the card he gave me. I looked at the place on the wall where he had sat and noticed black wisps of a large feather.

I got up and purposely walked to the white house. At the door, there was a little old lady bent and frail. I showed her the card and she told me to follow her. She took me through a series of dimly lit rooms, reminding me of tunnels, until we came to one at the end with large dusty windows. Heavy velvet curtains diffused the light. A woman looking like a Spanish doll was sitting at a table, her face was obscured by the black lace veil she wore. A large crystal ball sat on the table in front of her. Her voice was young and friendly, without looking at me she said, "come in Connie, and take a seat".

I sat opposite her and she gazed into the crystal ball. I

peered into it too, it seemed like there was fire inside the glass. She spoke again "you are conflicted Connie, you don't know which way to turn. There is a being inside you, you could love it and nurture it, it will change the course of your life, if that is what you want. Alternatively, you could let it go and leave the course of your life the way you planned it. The choice must be yours and yours alone, so you cannot blame any other for your decision. Leave now and don't return, unless you are sure you want to let it go".

Then the old lady reappeared, she tugged at my arm, she took me back through the dimly lit rooms and I was taken back out into the street.

Out on the road it was now twilight, the crickets chirped loudly around me. A Corbeau squawked loud and long above my head. The putrid smell of the La Basse dump filled my nostrils. I pulled my cardigan close and made my way home as quickly as I could with a strange sense of resolve.

Chapter 15

The exam room is at the end of the corridor, I rush in and take my seat, I'm almost late. The invigilator locks the doors. The clock above me ticks loudly it's 9am. I have an hour. I turn over the exam papers. I swish through the questions, panic is welling up inside of me, I can't understand what the questions mean. I didn't learn any of this. I look around but no-one else seems panicked. The girl on the right of me has her pen poised to write. The boy on the left of me is scribbling away, the scratch of his pen, scrapes at my fragile nerves. Confusion takes over, my mind is racing, my eyes dart around in panic.

The invigilator approaches, he is carrying something, he hands it to me. It's a chubby little baby screaming, his face is red and strained from the effort of emptying his lungs. The screaming sends shards of pain into my eardrums. I put my hands over my ears. "your baby needs feeding" the invigilator shouts above the screaming. All the students in the room turn around and stare at me.

Sounds from downstairs wake me, I sit up in bed sweat running down my back. The dream seemed so real, I can still hear the ticking of the exam clock, but it's just the clock on the side of my bed. I know now what I must do. I shower quickly. I catch a glance of my naked self in the mirror and I think of a young rose. I need to cut the bud off before it blooms, I think.

Downstairs, I feel like they are all looking at me, Ben, Toby and Gran. They seem to eye me suspiciously. I feel naked and exposed in their presence as if they are watching me too closely and know what I am about to do.

Outside the sun is bright and intense, but at last I can breathe easily. As I approach the white house, I'm filled with a sense of hope, a sense of resolve.

The old woman greets me at the door, as though she is expecting me. She leads me through the dimly lit tunnelled rooms. The spacious room at the end is bright and sunlight streams through the dusty windows. The table is gone and in its place, is a single bed. On a table, nearby are large silver polished implements. I look at what appears to be a large fork and a pair of forceps, but I look away quickly, not wanting to see more than I need to.

A middle-aged woman stands at the foot of the bed, her face is covered by a white surgical mask, her hair scooped high in a bun. She is wearing a long-striped apron, she reminds me of the butcher Mr Hardy, he wears a similar apron. I think she is the same lady but somehow older, whose face was obscured by the black veil, but I can't be sure.

"Connie" the masked woman says in a loud high-pitched voice, "take off your clothes and put this gown on". The old lady presents me with a small bamboo basket for my clothes and hands me what looks like a hospital gown. I change quickly and as discretely as I can, as the room provides no privacy. "Don't worry the masked woman laughs" no need to hide your body, we've seen it all before".

The old woman guides me onto the bed and pushes me gently to lie down. She opens my legs and hooks each of my feet into stirrups at the end of the bed. I stare numbly at my legs splayed wide, high above my head. The old woman pushes my gown up, over my waist, so my privates are exposed. Fears seeps into my soul, into my pores, into the pit of my stomach. I feel a prick of a needle and the room closes in and goes dark.

The invigilator pushes the baby towards me again "take it" he says "it's your baby isn't it?"

But I am confused I can't remember if it's my baby or not. I try to think hard but my mind is dense like a dark thick forest, I can't see or think through the trees.

The boy next to me stops writing he looks at me. "Is it your baby or not?" he sighs exasperated "it's not a trick question".

Everyone is focussed on me, big eyes staring. The room closes in. "I'm not sure, I don't think so" I say in a small voice, my mind is tangled, the nerves tight and curled.

The clock ticks loudly, I look up - it's 10am. "The exam is over" the invigilator shouts. I look through my exam booklet, the pages are blank, except at the top of the first page in my handwriting is written, CONNIE COSTELLO. WRONG ANSWER. YOU HAVE FAILED.

My eyes flicker open, I am in the large room with dusty windows again, I'm in my own clothes sitting on a deep chair that seems to swallow me up. The room is faded and I have to adjust my eyes to the lack of light. The large velvet curtains are drawn and a couple of table lamps strain to provide dim light.

The Spanish doll-like lady stands over me, her black lace veil masking her face. She extends her hand to me and says, "Go now Connie your burden has been taken from you".

The old woman appears, she places her hand on my shoulder and tugs me, I get up and turn to follow her out. Before I leave the room, I turn back quickly "I didn't pay you" I say.

The lady has her back turned to me, the side of her face is partially visible and in the poor light she momentarily looks like a corpse. She answers without turning "I have taken what I need, Connie, no need for further payment".

The old lady pulls on my sleeve urging me back through the tunnelled rooms. She opens the front door pushing me out briskly with her bony fingers. The front door is slammed shut.

The cool breeze brushes my face, the sound of rushing traffic surround and surprise me. It is dusk. Suddenly an excruciating pain, winds me, my stomach twists and churns in aching spasms. I bend down doubled in an effort to stop the terrible hurt. I stay like that bent and spent for what seems like eternity. When I rise slowly, the moon is casting an eerie gloom around me. The walled square is now quiet and serene.

I walk away slowly, every step a painful effort and my nose wrinkles to the stench of rotting flesh permeating from the La Basse dump behind. A cat wails mournfully in the distance.

Chapter 16

The next few days I continued to be in agony. My stomach churned in excruciating pain and I stayed in my bedroom as much as I could, hoping no one would notice my distress. Slowly the pain subsided and eventually time healed me, so that the whole episode of my pregnancy, dissolved into nothingness. Life returned to normal. I continued my loved-up relationship with Michael and as the start of University loomed, Martha and I made endless study plans and went on shopping expeditions to buy books and new clothes.

I was excited, a new chapter of my life had begun and I began to envisage myself as Dr Connie Costello. Martha had applied to study Fashion and Media at University and I had applied to do Medicine but albeit we were doing different degrees, we met often at lunch time on campus, to catch up and gossip. The course work was hard but I enjoyed the challenge of the research and the practical assignments. I was determined to do well and I studied hard. Martha and I made new friends at campus and we would hang around in groups to go to the library, the canteen or the bar.

A few times I came close to telling Martha about Michael but I always stopped short. Something was happening with Michael that I couldn't quite put my finger on. I loved him with all my heart, of that I was sure, but mixing with other students at University had shown me, another way of thinking, of speaking, of being. Unconsciously, I began to make comparisons between Michael and my friends at campus. Michael was lovely and kind and thoughtful but the realisation dawned on me that he was also common and uncouth. I tried hard to banish those thoughts out of my head, I chided myself for my snobbishness, but I couldn't help it. I was conflicted, because at the same time the thought of being without Michael was intolerable, he was part of me and I came to depend on him. I knew I had been neglecting him of late, due to my studies so I became determined to be a better and more attentive girlfriend.

During the Christmas holidays I spent a lot of time with Michael and one cloudy morning Michael got up early to work on a car, he kissed me goodbye and I left his annex, to go home. On the way out, I met his father Mr Moore on the porch, he said it looked like rain was on its way and invited me in to have breakfast with himself and Mrs Moore. I reluctantly accepted not knowing how to decline without seeming rude. I didn't really know them that well and I thought it would be weird eating with them without Michael by my side.

We sat in the covered porch, while Mrs Moore brought out fried plantain, salt-fish and fried bakes. We made some small talk, until Mr Moore said, "tell us about your University, Connie, Michael tell us yuh real bright". So I told them about my assignments, the physical experiments, the dissertation, the lectures. Maybe I talked too much out of nervousness or went into too much detail, but after a short while I found them both zoning out, as they feigned understanding.

While we ate and spoke, I made observations. Michael's Dad was tall and broad like Michael, but he had a pot belly and his hair was thinning on top. The shirt he wore was too tight and short for him, highlighting the roundness of his tummy even more. Michael's Mum was thin and worn, her hair was tied in a bun and was streaked with grey. Her thin cotton dress revealed flat, worn out, drooped breasts, which seemed to end at her waist. She may have been pretty once, but she had let herself go, as though her looks were now irrelevant. I noticed latterly that the table she served the breakfast on, was actually an old wooden crate turned upside down.

On the way home, I replayed the scene in my head and not knowing quite why, I found the whole experience disturbing.

University life was fun but hard at the same time and as the exams came near, Martha and I spent all our hours studying. In the library one sunny afternoon Martha had a pen in her mouth as she stared into space.

"Hey what are you thinking about?" I asked concerned.

"Oh nothing" she beamed "I was just thinking that soon we would have completed one whole academic year here and the time has flown past, soon we will have our degrees and we will be well on our way to our perfect lives".

I considered what she said and then probed

"Martha do you think we could ever be happy and have our perfect lives if we fell in love with boys from the village?"

Martha looked at me thoughtful, she looked down at her feet and responded "actually Connie there is a boy I saw that I quite like the look of in the village but I have pushed him out of my mind, because let's face it" she paused she reached out and grabbed my hand "let's face it, Connie, for what we want to achieve, like success in our careers, to travel the world and to have big fancy houses and cars, these country boys can't give that to us".

I considered what she said and heard myself answer vaguely "Yes Martha, you're right".

I looked at Martha, she had her head buried back in a book and all I could think about was the old crate box, turned upside down and used as a table. Worry crept over me and I felt hollow in the pit of my stomach.

A few weeks before the exams, I decided to tell Michael that I would not be able to see him for a few weeks until the exams were over. He suggested that we meet at a new Thai restaurant in town as a treat, as we would not be seeing each other for a while. The restaurant was posh, all glass and glitter balls and oriental music played softly in the background, giving a serene ambiance. As usual Michael was attentive, he was dressed smartly, his long wavy hair hung loose in glossy chunks and he was clean shaven, he looked very handsome. I could see other women looking at him when we walked to our table and I buzzed with pride because he was mine. I decided there and then to tell Martha all about him, the next time I saw her. I beamed with a glow of happiness as we ordered. As we chatted, I really looked at Michael and realisation dawned on me that he was the whole package kind, loving, thoughtful and handsome, what more could I want.

We ate and drank, laughed and joked but halfway through the evening something changed. I began to feel a bit uneasy when I noticed that Michael had become a bit tense, he began glancing around nervously and became sullen.

Eventually he looked me in the eye and blurted out too loud "Connie!"

I held his gaze and I could see that his eyes were wet. He continued more softly and slowly "Connie, you know I love you dearly and I know you love me, but sometimes love just isn't enough, I can't give you what you want".

He continued to speak to me, he took my hand, but my brain shut down, numb. At first, I couldn't understand what was happening but then the light bulb in my brain turned on and tears blurred my vision and shock took over. Conversations began to swirl around me. Voices all at once echoed, I could not hear, great chunks of words were lost, as Michael continued to speak and look down at his hands. Before I knew what was happening I began to snivel, I heard myself begging him not to break up with me, I was pathetic as I heard myself pleading "please don't do this Michael, we can work this out".

Michael looked at me sympathetically he had resumed his composure, he was no longer tearful. He said thoughtfully, "I see the way you have changed since you went to Uni, the way you look at me, the way you look at my parents, you don't mean to, I know that, but you look down on us".

The room came back into focus and Michael continued "Connie the things about me that don't make you happy are not going to change, I'm not going in the direction you are going in, so there is no future for us".

My mind drifted off again, on what could have been, of Michael and our baby, a happy life. Michael was the love of my life and even as Michael sat opposite me, I began to mourn our relationship and his place in my life.

Michael's voice came back to me in waves "I know this is hard for you, Connie, it's hard for me too, but I'm just doing what you have found too hard to do yourself".

Outside the restaurant, the air was warm and a hound of dogs, howled loudly in the background. "I will always love you Connie Costello", Michael said as he smiled sadly. I stood there unsteady, looking up at him lost for words, my handsome ex-boyfriend. I couldn't move or speak. I felt bereft of emotion. Time stood still as we were cocooned in a capsule of prolonged silence. Then Michael embraced me in his large muscular arms and hugged me to him. I smelt the familiar scents of him and collapsed in his arms, big guffawing cries of pain coming out of me.

As I walked home grief drained out of me through waves of tears. I felt like I was at the edge of an abyss, trying hard not to fall in.

Chapter 17

I was in emotional turmoil I was lost without Michael, I yearned for him. But after the yearning subsided, anger took over. How dare he dump me, who the hell did he think he was. I was going places and he was just a motor mechanic. He had done me a favour, I tried to convince myself over and over but the pain and hurt told me otherwise.

A week later I was at Martha's house studying for the exams and she was talking about our perfect life plan. We talked about where we would live, the type of house we would design and have built for ourselves, the countries we would live in and visit. So many times I came close to telling her all about Michael, how we met, our deep romance and how he broke my heart and dumped me, but once again something stopped me.

One evening I got home from Martha's and the house had a very bad atmosphere, there was complete silence as I entered. Ben and Toby were seated upright on the settee, looking at me expectantly. Gran was in the kitchen and as she heard me enter she shouted, "Connie take a seat" I could hear at once that Gran was in a bad mood. My heart immediately began to do summersaults, I thought for sure, that she'd found out about me and Michael. I felt light headed, the room began to spin and my heart pounded against my chest.

Gran came in from the kitchen wiping her hands on a tea towel, her face was set hard. She plonked herself down on a chair next to me. I was trying to think straight, to think of good excuses. Maybe I could say that Gran was mistaken and that Michael was Ben's friend not mine! I could legitimately say now that I wasn't seeing Michael, it wasn't all untrue, as we had really broken up.

Gran sighed hard she looked at us with narrowed eyes "look kids there's no easy way to say this".

My heart was pounding so hard against my chest wall, I thought Gran could hear it.

Gran continued "you won't be seeing your Mother for a while, I can't have her back in this house. She is a complete disgrace, yuh know she forget my son already, my lovely handsome son, yuh father! She take up with a next man already and she move in with he! My son is not even cold in his grave!"

Toby's eyes stretched wide, he looked visibly distressed and asked, "Gran are you saying that Mum can't come to visit us anymore?"

Gran got up and shouted at Toby "No! She can't set foot in this house again, she's betrayed your father in the eyes of the lord, she's taken another man!"

I looked at Ben and he glowered back at me, suddenly Ben got up, anger seemed to emanate from his pores. He approached Gran and Gran's eyes betrayed a type of fear, as she saw him approach her. His face was stern, pure rage outwardly showing. He raised his hand as if to strike Gran and held his hand inches from Gran's face. Ben said in a low voice "don't ever speak about my mother like that again you old witch, don't you realise our father died five years ago".

Toby gasped loudly and stood up quickly, he hopped about awkwardly "Ben please don't hit Gran" he almost shouted.

Ben eyed Toby, then he sneered at Gran but his body seemed to relax a bit, he dropped his hand and ran up the stairs, the muscles in his neck were bulging and tears streamed angrily down his face.

The next few days carried on in the same vein with Gran and Ben arguing constantly and then there were the silent days where Gran and Ben ignored each other. Toby and I were caught in the middle, listening to Gran moaning about Ben how he was rude and ungrateful and then listening to Ben moaning about Gran how she was a cold heartless witch. Naturally we always took Ben's side without making it obvious to Gran. One-day Gran called us all to attention again. We all sat in the sitting room patiently waiting and thinking about what we'd done wrong this time. There was always something we had done wrong. Gran seemed to be prevaricating, she made us wait for ages before she sat down with us. Once seated she sighed deeply and seemed to struggle to get the words out, before she revealed that she could no longer cope with Ben and that she had made plans to send him to England to live with our father's brother Hector.

Upon hearing the news Toby jumped up and put his arms around Ben's neck, small tears streamed down his young face "no please, Gran" he pleaded "please don't send Ben away, he's our brother, we've already lost Mum and Dad, the three of us need to stay together now, please, Gran" he snivelled.

My heart peeled, I felt numb, it was always the three of us against the world. I tried to speak but a ball caught in my throat and I felt paralysed. I looked at Ben, he looked stoic, his eyes stared ahead blankly as though he wasn't really present.

That night I went into Ben's room, his eyes were glazed and he lay silently on top of his bed. I asked him if he was ok, he shrugged nonchalantly. I asked him what he thought about going to England but he didn't respond. After some time, I realised that Toby had quietly slipped into the room and was holding my hand. We watched Ben in silence, he seemed broken. I looked at Ben on his bed, I noticed as though for the first time, the old-fashioned mahogany wardrobe and the damp patch on the ceiling, the silence seemed to penetrate everything around us. Then Ben looked up at us, sadness etched on his face and said quietly "you two please go now and leave me alone". Toby let go of my hand and walked around the bed and placed his hand on Ben's shoulder, I could see tears forming at the corners of Ben's eyes "Toby please leave me alone" Ben shouted.

The next few days no-one really spoke, dinners were the usual silence but we didn't even bother to pass notes to each other anymore. Everyone seemed lost in their own worlds. Subtly though Gran was pursuing the plan, the one-way plane ticket arrived and a suitcase appeared in the hallway.

Coming home from college was like entering a cold war zone, I just wanted to run away. A week after Gran's announcement, I got home from college my mind awash with the latest exam, but before I opened the front door I could hear Gran sobbing loudly. My first thought was that Ben had lost his temper again and had hit her this time. Inside the house the sobbing was melodramatic, big loud sighs and wailing. At that moment, I resented Gran. I bet Ben just pushed her, and she was making a big deal out of it, she was so over the top. Then Ben appeared he looked scared, his eyes were red rimmed. "Oh God, Ben" I gasped "what did you do to her". Ben's lips quivered, he suddenly looked gaunt, he grabbed me to him and began to cry, in heartfelt sobs.

I was shocked I couldn't understand what he had done, I pulled away from him and looked into his face, his tears flowed without pause and he collapsed in a heap on the floor. My heart sank as I suddenly remembered Selassi and the way Ben had pushed him, the past snapped up to meet me and fear crept up and grabbed at my heart. I was really beginning to get scared now. I ran upstairs not knowing what state I'd find Gran in.

I found Gran slumped on her bed sitting up awkwardly, I couldn't at first glance see any outward sign of injury on her. As I approached her, she gave me a sideward glance and began to sob gently. Then she looked up at me, she suddenly looked a hundred years old. "Gran, what happened" I whispered.

"Oh, Gawd Connie" she bawled "it's Toby - he's dead".

The sun was shining too brightly through the bedroom window, I could feel the warmth stinging my face. This couldn't be right. The sun wouldn't be shining if Toby were dead.

My mind felt heavy and weary, thoughts rushed around not making any sense. I approached Gran, a tentative smile forming on my face "don't talk rubbish, Gran - what are you saying, you're not making any sense".

Gran looked at me with a sad grimace on her face. "Toby is dead child," she said in a tired voice "he got hit by a car on the way home from school. This family is cursed".

The sun slapped my face with a stinging sensation, the room began to spin and tilt beneath me, the ground seemed to rise up to meet me, as my head hit the floor.

Chapter 18

The next few days were a blur, I woke up every day on a tear stained pillow, to find Ben at the end of my bed, his eyes swollen into slits. When I tried to get up I was unsteady on my feet, the world seemed tilted, my head felt woolly. Downstairs there were people all around, Mum, Mr Sookoo and his family from next door, Ruby and Shanti, Kelvin and Harry, various aunts and uncles and other cousins. There was wailing and bawling and lots of chatter and food being cooked. Gran had taken to her bed for most of the days.

It was all unbearable, the people, the cooking, the noise. The absence of Toby was like a lacuna in my stomach, everything gone, his wide eyes, his cheeky smile, the touch of his small hand in mine. Everything reminded me of him, of his goodness, his sadness and his laughter. I wanted to dwell in my private memories of him, but the noise and the chatter of people, their crying and their sobs invaded my privacy.

Mum was a mess, she was distraught and haggard, she looked close to death herself. She held Ben and I close to her and made an excruciatingly painful sound like it was coming from deep inside a wounded animal. She apologised to us over and over for being a useless mother who had let us all down. This was her punishment she said, the karma for her sins. "When I lost your Dad, I still had all of you lovely children around me, it should have been enough, but I loved the inside of a rum bottle more, I lost the way and took the wrong path, and now it's too late to turn back, the other path is no longer available" Mum said wistfully as she sobbed her heart out.

Shanti wore the pain on her face like a contorted palsy, the sorrow seemed twisted into her features. I was surprised that even the shallow and insincere Ruby seemed genuinely bereaved. Her signature red lipstick was abandoned and she looked uncertain and shocked. At one point, she smiled at me sadly and said, "I can't imagine what you and Ben are going through, because for the first time in my life I feel real sorrow deep in my heart"

The funeral was too hard to recall: -

The Lord Is My Shepherd was being played by the organist, the white coffin was taken from the hurst and carried down the aisle by our cousins Kelvin, Harry and Ronald on one side and Ben, Shanti's Dad and Mr Sookoo on the other side. I recalled my horror as the coffin seemed to almost topple over, when Ben lost his footing and momentarily lost his grip. I remember feeling sick as the pungent smell of the wreaths permeated everything around. The wreaths smelt of death, as they spelt the words - SON, TOBY, BROTHER, COUSIN.

Toby's friends from his class got up to read their individualised bidding prayers. Ramone said a prayer that he made up himself. Mum sobbed her way through as she read a poem about Toby still being all around in the wind and sky. Ruby and Shanti both did readings from the bible. Me, Mum and Ben sat on the front pew of the church and held hands.

Then when I didn't think it could get any worse, Gran got up unexpectedly and walked towards the pulpit. She smiled at the priest who looked confused and she raised her hand and said, "I just want to say a few words". The priest nodded his consent.

Gran looked old but she stood tall and straight as she looked at the full congregation. She opened her bag and took out a few crumpled pages. Silence descended on the church in anticipation. She cleared her throat and began.

"Toby was my Grandson" she paused and glared at Mum "you all know only too well that his Mother Serena didn't deserve him, she didn't deserve any of her children, but Toby in particular was special".

I looked at Mum and squeezed her hand, she stifled back tears, dabbing at her eyes with a paper tissue which was disintegrating. Ben put his arms around Mum and glared at Gran.

Gran cleared her throat again and continued. "Toby like his father was a good pure soul. He was goodness personified. He was only fifteen years old, too young to die but too good to carry on living in this God forsaken wicked world. They say God takes back the good ones first and that is why Toby had to return to heaven. God does not take back the ones that spread their legs and get pregnant out of wedlock".

At this comment, she glared at Shanti and Shanti quickly looked down.

Gran continued "God does not take back the vain and profane". At this comment she glared at Ruby. Ruby held Gran's gaze and kissed her lips loudly, as she flicked her hair and exaggeratedly pouted her red lipstick lips.

Gran then stared at Ben as she said, "and God does not take back the rude and ungrateful".

At this point the congregation began shifting uneasily in their seats and the priest looked uncertain and worried, but Gran continued

"That's why Toby had to go back to heaven, he was too

good for this world. This is a world where evil spirits lurk in dark corners doing the devil's work. Toby's soul was too good to be surrounded by such evil. Now Toby is back in heaven with his Daddy and his dog, Bandit and he is happy. He is without worry, without sadness and without pain. Toby will always be with us in our hearts guiding us and showing us the right way to live. Eternal rest grant to him Oh lord and let perpetual light shine upon him. Amen".

At last the organist began playing *Abide With Me* and the congregation got up to leave the church.

At the graveside Mum fainted twice as the coffin was lowered into the ground. All the mourners threw white roses onto the coffin, and then we all grabbed handfuls of the brown dry claylike mud and threw that on top of the coffin too. After that it was all a bit vague, endless prayers and hymns and crying and pain. Pain that pulls at your core to create that feeling of profound sadness.

The worst part was when the funeral was over and everyone went home and what was left was me, Ben and Gran at home, weary and melancholy. Worst still was that two days later, Ben was on a plane to England and I would not see him again for several years.

The day before Ben left we talked late into the night. Ben berated himself for shouting at Toby to leave him alone, just before Toby died. Ben said he couldn't forgive himself. He had however made up his mind to make the most of going to England, Sarah would be going to University in London soon and they would at least have each other again.

The day that Ben left, the taxi driver, told us that he had recently driven the Lady who had knocked Toby over. He said that she had lost her mind over killing Toby. As he put Ben's suitcase in the car, he said the Lady kept saying over and over that she was driving and all of a sudden, a massive black Corbeau appeared in the road in front of the car, the wings spread out wide, which caused her to brake and swerve to avoid hitting the bird. She felt she'd hit something and thought it was the bird but when she got out of the car, she realised that she'd hit Toby by mistake instead. The Lady said when she looked around the bird seemed to have disappeared, she said she had not even noticed Toby before the car hit him.

My brain felt too tired to properly digest the information.

Once Ben left, I felt bereft of any feelings, sadness flowed through my veins deadening any real emotion. I never returned to University and never finished my exams. Gran and I shared the same house but what little bond there was seemed irretrievably strained. Gran did not shout at me to get up, get dressed, go to Uni. She just left me to sleep most of the day and then walk about Toby and Ben's rooms in my night clothes aimlessly sitting on their empty beds. As the days turned into weeks, a black mist settled on me, the outside world lost any meaning and my mind was too weary to think. The urge to cry came and went without any thought, I found myself re-living memories of the loss of Daddy, loss of Bandit, loss of Toby. The pang of loss, kicked me in the stomach many times over, winding me each time. I didn't feel the need to eat, I had no appetite, the shredding of my heart was enough to fill me up.

Chapter 19

My perfect life was a joke, I'd lost everything, Daddy, Michael, Toby and Ben even Mum was not around for any real emotional support.

Martha came around often, she tried to cheer me up, she encouraged me to return to University. She didn't understand that I felt a real pain in the pit of my stomach, which drained away any hope. I couldn't contemplate doing anything which would require any effort on my part. Martha's constant attempt to make me see life more positively, got on my nerves and I pushed her away. Her life was still on the right trajectory, her perfect life was still in view, whereas mine was a shambles.

One rainy day I heard Mr Sookoo on the porch talking to Gran in hushed tones, I knew they were talking about me, I heard him say "she looks like a skeleton, she's just a shell of the girl she was".

The next day Mr Sookoo and Gran called me downstairs, they said I needed to pull myself together and that Mr Sookoo found me an apprenticeship in a pharmaceutical company and I would be starting on Monday. At first, I protested. I said I wasn't ready, I needed time to grieve. Gran said I already had three months to grieve and that if I wanted to keep living in her house I had to get a job.

So, it was decided that I would start work, despite my protests. On Monday morning Gran woke me up early, she picked a black dress for me to wear, directed me to get showered and changed, she made me breakfast and then she pushed me out of the door and handed me the address of my new job and directions to get there. On the bus, I aimlessly gazed out of the window, I felt outrage and injustice. I was on my own now without both my brothers, I was virtually an orphan and now I had to earn my keep. I thought of the story of Cinderella and felt an affinity with a fairy tale, which was turning into my reality.

As I approached the address, I was impressed to find that the building was a large imposing glass structure. The interior was just as impressive plush and modern with lots of reflective and stone surfaces, everything looked brand new. I was directed to the third floor to meet the Director Anna Soucan. I was very surprised to see that she was fairly young, I estimated in her early thirties and she was extremely attractive. She got up from behind her desk and greeted me with a firm handshake. She was wearing a tight cream tailored trousers suit which showed off her curvaceous figure. The cream silk blouse underneath showed strain from her full bosom. A gold choker style necklace hung around her long slender neck. Her long shiny wavy black hair, framed her sculptured face, which was line free. Her smile revealed white straight teeth and highlighted her high glossy cheekbones. Her bowtie shaped lips were full and painted red. But her eyes made me feel exposed, as though she could read my thoughts, she had large bright black eyes set deep, and when she looked at me, they seemed to penetrate right into my soul. When she extended her hand to shake mine, I noticed beautiful long fingers and perfectly manicured red nails. She took my breath away and was like no-one I had ever met before, sensual but very professional, all rolled up into one gorgeous being.

She explained that my job would be to process the orders from pharmacies and deliver some of those orders on occasion. As a result of the delivery side of the job, the company would pay for me to get my driver's licence. A tiny spark of joy spiked through my gloom, I'd always wanted to learn to drive and here was my perfect opportunity.

Anna then took me to meet two ladies, as she called them, called Trisha and Nora. Trisha was blonde with a perfect tan and Nora was a deep chocolate brown all over. They were both gorgeous, all glossy pouty lips and long legs. They both welcomed me and helpfully showed me the ropes.

That evening when I got home, I felt deflated, I looked down at my flat shoes and dowdy black dress, my hair was pulled back in a high tight pony tail, I looked positively frumpy. I was also disillusioned by Gran's reaction to my getting a driving licence, instead of being happy for me, she was appalled. She said women had no place driving motor cars, she said that driving was a man's job and was not feminine, she instructed me to decline that part of the job. Gran's attitude made my gloom feel palpable. I wanted to moan about her to Ben and Toby, I wanted to pass notes to them about her around the dinner table. I was patently lonely, all on my own with my witch of a Granny.

But going to work was a tonic and slowly my spirits lifted, seeing Anna, Nora and Trisha every day made me aspire to be like them, beautiful and confident. I decided to ignore Granny's advice and live my life for me. I took up the driving lessons (what Granny didn't know, couldn't offend her) and I vowed to change my life starting with buying some nice clothes and make up, with my first wage packet.

As soon as I got paid I bought a new grey coloured dress

which showed off my legs, a matching pair of high heels and some make-up. I didn't have much money left over but I thought it was worth it. I decided to buy a new outfit every week for five weeks and then I could wear the outfits on one day each week and always look smart.

Much to the annoyance of Gran, every morning I got up early to do my make-up and hair to perfection, coupled with my new outfits, I had turned into a corporate looking chick. Trisha and Nora were very impressed, they said I looked totally different, they gave me beauty tips and shared office gossip with me. The three of us became good friends and they showed me how to party and have a good time. Over time my sadness began to float away, but I felt a gnawing guilt every time I felt happy. Deep down I felt as if I had to wear my sadness as a badge of honour in memory of Toby and Daddy, in case I forgot my loss. I tried to explain my tangle of feelings to Trisha and Nora, to make sense of it all.

"You've had a sad life up to now, Connie" Nora said in a motherly tone "but it doesn't mean the rest of your life has to be filled with sadness, it's time to start having fun, there's no point worrying about the past when your future beckons!"

"I can better that advice" piped Trisha "I read somewhere, life is a banquet to be savoured, like a melt in your mouth creamy toffee fudge, so start savouring Connie!"

Chapter 20

Trisha and Nora teased me and said that my new look had caught the attention of the office manager Nick Murphy, a fact of which I was not totally oblivious.

I had noticed Nick around the office, he floated around speaking to people and sitting at his desk, I was told he was the office manager but I never gave him much thought. But over time I had become aware of his glances and smiles. Although we worked in the same office we barely spoke at all. He seemed to me a very shy person and his shyness made me nervous. He smiled at me awkwardly and I found it difficult to maintain eye contact with him without feeling uneasy.

After months of working together and barely saying two words to each other, I found it odd when one day he randomly asked me out for a date. Trisha and Nora encouraged me to give him a chance, they told me he was a good catch, he was from a rich family and he seemed kind. But I was not attracted to him at all, so I politely declined and told him I was not ready to start dating. His reaction to my rejection surprised me, his face became pale and his eyes blinked back disbelief, like a wide-eyed child confused and totally thrown by my refusal of him. He took a moment to process what had happened, he paused as his eyes darted around rapidly, under his wide black rimmed glasses. Then he said quietly "Oh, OK".

As he turned to walk away, he paused again his back bent like a stringed puppet, but then he straightened up and asked innocent and child-like "would you mind if I ask you again in a few months?"

I was warmed by his honest unashamed lack of pride. There was something endearing about him. "Sure" I was surprised to hear myself say. As he walked away, I turned to see Nora and Trisha both giving me approving looks.

On the way home I admitted to myself that the truth was I didn't want to get involved with anyone. I was enjoying my new-found freedom, of driving, of being financially independent, of being carefree and enjoying life. But most of all the hurt of being unceremoniously dumped by Michael still felt raw and still throbbed like an unhealed wound. I knew I was vulnerable to being broken again, vulnerable to being hurt. It was easier to stay single and enjoy life without exposing myself to more hurt and upset. The hurt of losing Daddy and Toby and of missing Ben, Michael and Mum made me crave a hedonistic existence, devoid of deep emotion. My plan was to keep myself protected, I would keep away from relationships.

But after the first encounter with Nick, we seemed to keep bumping into each other at the photocopier, in the car park, in the canteen and we began to exchange pleasantries and then we had short conversations. Nora and Trisha were pleased but I told them not to get excited because I didn't have feelings for him. It was true, there were no sparks flying. He seemed lonely and I felt sorry for him, so I made an effort to speak to him and I found him very easy to talk to. There was something about his manner and his voice that I found soothing. We slowly got to know each other. Eventually I started noticing that he was a lovely human being, he was thoughtful and responsible, he wasn't lonely as I had first thought, he had a small group of loyal friends. He was close to his parents, he was an only child and maybe that is why he seemed mature beyond his years and confident in himself. He was clear about his goals, he wanted to do well for the company, he wanted a family, he wanted his parents to become grandparents, so they could shower the love they had given to him, to his own children. He was a big kid, he wanted to run on the beach with his kids and take them to the funfair. He had a great strength of character and I realised he would make a great husband. But I convinced myself that I didn't have feelings for him and I didn't find him attractive.

Nora and Trisha said I had fallen for him but I told them he didn't turn my world upside down. Nora looked at me in her motherly way and said, "girl, sometimes the flame that starts slow burns the brightest".

Trisha piped up "I can better that, sometimes when you have been hurt before, you don't want to get too excited about a new love, in case you get hurt again. So, your heart makes you fall in love slowly, so you don't notice, until you realise, this love is all the more real".

A few months later he asked me on a date again, I agreed this time and had to admit to myself at this stage, that I had started to have feelings for him. We spent the night together at his house, neither of us expected sex and so we just talked. We opened up to each other about all our hopes and fears, I told him things I had always kept to myself, I wondered if he would think I was crazy but he didn't. It was so natural and nice, we talked until we heard the cockerels crowing and we realised the sun was rising. As we kissed each other goodbye I knew my heart was taken.

It happened so slowly that before I realised, I had let myself become vulnerable around him, I fell in love. I slowly realised how much better life was with him in it and when he asked me to marry him, there was no hesitation when I said a resounding yes.

The wedding day was the best day of my life. I was blissfully happy. My dress was the epitome of beautiful, an ivory fitted mermaid shaped off the shoulder designer number. Nick's mother planned it all with meticulous detail. It was a big Catholic wedding in the Cathedral. There were Rolls Royce cars for me and my bridesmaids and a big Bentley for Nick and his best man and page boys. There were flowers everywhere in the church, pink and white roses on the pulpit and on every pew. The reception was in the Hilton hotel and again there were flowers everywhere. Even the drinks coasters had our names and date of marriage inscribed on them. The chairs were dressed in white silk and tied with pink and white bows to match the bouquets. Everything was perfect but it was the smallest and unexpected things that brought me the most joy and made the day memorable. Every time I glanced at my Nick my heart skipped a beat, he was so deliriously happy and I felt like the luckiest girl alive. Mum and Gran came with Ben who had flown over from England. Nick had insisted on paying for his flight. Nick and his parents had also insisted on paying for our special guests to stay the night of the wedding at the Hilton, Mum and

Gran were delighted. It was amazing to see Mum and Gran getting on well. Mum whispered in my ear "Connie, well done, you made it to the big time!" and Gran congratulated me by saying "Connie I'm so glad you found a good Catholic boy".

Nick's father and his best man, did long funny speeches. Nick's Mum cried happy tears when his father said they hadn't lost a son but gained a daughter. Ben stood up and called for a toast to his beautiful and resilient sister. Then Anna stood up to raise a toast, I could sense all the men ogling her, she looked radiant oozing something which made me think of profanity. She raised her glass and said "well done to Connie, let's raise a toast, she's bagged herself a kind, loving man, who shows her respect", she smiled at me briefly, while everyone clapped loudly. I watched as her eyes lingered on Nick and she smiled at him tenderly.

Trisha, Nora and Martha were my bridesmaids and they all looked outstanding. They hugged me and congratulated me. I felt blessed to have all my best friends in one place. I noticed Shanti and her husband Charles and Rosie and Preston and they came over after the speeches to congratulate us. Everything went to plan and happiness flowed like the good champagne that Nick's Dad was happily pouring, like water.

During the first dance, I held on to Nick tight, and when he kissed me tenderly I couldn't believe that life could be so good to me. Ben asked me to dance and he looked at me with pride, I hugged him close, he had bloomed into a handsome and sturdy man. He told me Nick was a descent chap, "he will treat you right through thick and thin" he beamed.

Just before Nick and I left for our honeymoon, Martha called out to me, she ran up to me and hugged me. "Connie, I'm so happy for you, do you remember our promise to achieve the perfect life, well Connie your perfect life starts here".

In the taxi on the way to the airport I held Nick's hand and said a silent prayer. *Dear God, I have endured such tragedy so far, thank you for my perfect life, long may it continue, Amen".*

Chapter 21

God seemed on my side, because the first year of marriage was pure bliss. Nick's parents bought us a plush apartment which looked out onto the northern range mountains. It was bright and modern but Nick put me in charge of decorating it. I got such joy from choosing fabrics and paint colours, that I even lived and breathed interior design in my sleep. We continued to work at the pharmaceutical company and had both been given expensive company cars by Anna as part of our wedding present. We often held dinner parties, where I practiced my culinary skills. But more often than not Nick insisted on caterers so I could pamper myself before the parties. Trisha and Nora were frequent visitors and we all enjoyed pampering days together.

Within quick succession Trisha and Nora both met the men of their dreams, so Nick and I found ourselves involved in the happy preparations of planning weddings and celebrations. Our social circle grew and us three couples spent a lot of time together. Life was good.

After about a year I got a metallic taste in my mouth, I'd got that taste before and I instinctively knew I was pregnant. But I had to be sure so I had it confirmed by the doctor, before I told Nick. When I told Nick, he was like the cat that got the cream, his eyes twinkled with delight, he picked me up and spun me around and around. We decided to keep it a secret for the first eight weeks, we didn't want to tempt fate by announcing our good news too soon.

Nick was ecstatic, he said we should make every day a new adventure. He said it was important to project positive feelings onto the baby as my body was creating a precious life. He didn't want me to get overwhelmed by anything and he made sure I looked after myself. He stocked up on green vegetables and citrus fruits, whole grains, and healthy fats and bought me folic acid tablets. He bought baby magazines and we read them together. I realised that this was my first awesome experience, yes, I felt sick, but this was more than offset as we decided to spend quality time with the tiny miracle growing inside me every day. We sang to the baby in our terrible voices, we talked incessantly about all the things we would do together. We played music toward my belly. Nick was convinced that classical music developed a baby's brain and he played Beethoven's Romance No.2, every day. Through Beethoven I began to breathe and connect to our baby through meditation. I felt a beautiful deep connection with the baby, I felt and imagined invisible bonds holding us together. I was filled with a sense of peaceful joy.

As soon as we had the eight-week scan, we announced it to the world. Anna allowed me to work part-time and on my days off I took up pre-natal massages and yoga. We were downright blissful. The scan picture was pinned proudly on our notice board.

We read in a magazine that writing a pregnancy journal, noting the changes in my body and my feelings, was therapeutic, so I began to do that as a daily ritual. I was in a truly happy and healthy frame of mind.

One day at work, Trisha was so excited, she announced her news in a squeal. "I'm pregnant too, Connie", she said as she cuddled me. Thereafter we talked nothing but pregnancy. Nora was a bit jealous we could tell, she gave us sideways glances and her smiles seemed superficial. One-day Nora blurted out "oh gosh you two, can't you change the subject, it's getting boring talking babies, every day! Even Anna is sick of it".

Trisha shouted back "don't be so negative Nora, soon it will happen to you, we are just happy, don't you understand, it's a miracle, our bodies are creating new lives!"

The next day Trisha called me aside, she said that she was feeling negative vibes from Nora and especially Anna, she said that we should distance ourselves from them, as negative energy could negatively affect our babies. "We have to create boundaries, we don't have energy for unimportant things, we need to focus on creating a healthy baby, imagine holding our beautiful babies in our arms" she said.

When Trisha got to her eighth week of pregnancy, she asked Anna if she could work part-time so she could rest a bit and join me at pre-natal yoga and massage classes. As soon as Trisha came out of Anna's office, I could see she was upset. As she passed my desk, she whispered "let's meet for lunch".

I couldn't wait for lunchtime and as soon as the clock struck noon, I headed towards the canteen. A hand grabbed mine, I saw it was Trisha, "no" she said, "we need to talk outside the office today". As we walked out of the building, I saw Anna watching us, she looked sensually beautiful as usual. Her red lips seemed bloodlike.

Trisha walked about ten minutes to a restaurant. I was perturbed to see that it was near the walled square, opposite the white house, where I had my back-street abortion. I felt sick, I didn't want to be reminded of that time. We sat down and ordered, Trisha looked around nervously and jumped every time the restaurant door opened. The smell of fried food made me feel nauseous.

Trisha looked at me, she looked frightened. "Well naturally Anna turned me down, she won't let me work part-time, she says you are already working part-time and she has to think of the business needs. She says that there's too much work and she can't spare me".

I felt guilty and wondered if Trisha was angry with me, she seemed really upset. "Oh, I'm so sorry Trisha" I said genuinely.

"There's something I must tell you Connie, Nora and I were going to tell you when you first started but then you got together with Nick and well, Nick and Anna are really good friends, so we didn't tell you in the end".

My heart started to race, I couldn't imagine what it could be but I could see that Trisha was scared. I didn't know what to say, but then Trisha continued:

"Look this is going to sound crazy, there's no easy way of saying this, so I'm just going to tell you, Anna is evil she's a devil woman!"

I choked and laughed, "are you kidding me?" I asked, but I could see the fear in Trisha's eyes and I knew she believed what she'd said.

"No, I'm deadly serious, she is the most beautiful woman I've ever seen, have you seen anyone as beautiful as her, ever, just think about it?"

"No" I answered it was true I had never seen anyone as mesmerizingly beautiful.

"Exactly" Trisha said "but it's not natural, she gets her beauty from the underworld, from sorcery. Don't get too close to her, she will ruin you, don't ever look too deeply into her eyes, if you look deep in her eyes she will draw you in by her beauty and then she will suck away your hopes and dreams. She gets her beauty from sleeping with the devil. She's really an old hag but she sheds her old skin to become new and young and beautiful every day. She goes out at night, she flies around as a black crow or as a ball of fire and sucks the blood of victims, she gets into their homes through the keyhole or under the doors, as she can change her shape and make herself very small. The blood she sucks makes her young and beautiful".

I was taken aback "but how would you know this?" I said, incredulous.

Trisha looked around and lowered her voice "well one night, about two years ago, I went out with some friends and as I was going home, I realised that I'd forgotten my house keys in the office. I contacted Nick and he drove to meet me and took me to the office. Nick opened the doors and deactivated the alarm but he waited downstairs for me. I ran up the stairs as quickly as I could because the office was dark and it felt gloomy. I saw my keys on my desk and I grabbed them but as I was about to go back downstairs, I heard a noise coming from Anna's office. I crept up to the door because I thought it was a burglar, but when I looked in I saw Anna, except it wasn't Anna it was an old woman with Anna's features. On the chair near her desk looked like a coat of young skin. I was so scared, I ran down the stairs as quick as I could. Luckily when I got downstairs Nick was talking on his phone, I shouted to him that I'd got my keys and I ran all the way home. I never believed in any black magic before that, but as soon as I got home I called my Mum and she told me to put a large bowl of rice outside my front door every night for the rest of my life, as that was the only way I could protect myself. My Mum said that the creature will not enter because they are obligated to gather up every single grain of rice before dawn. The creature will not bother, because doing that will take up too much time and they risk being seen".

"Anyway" Trisha continued "the next day, I told Nora and I was surprised, when she said she had already figured it out, I asked her how she knew and she said that Anna always wore long dresses or trouser suits so you could never see her cloven feet. Ask Nora if you don't believe me".

As we left the air-conditioned restaurant the sun seemed far too bright and far too hot and I swooned with exhaustion.

Chapter 22

A few days later I decided to ask Nick about Anna. As we sat down to a healthy baby friendly dinner, I nonchalantly said "Anna is very beautiful - is she married?"

Nick looked at me suspiciously, "are you getting jealous about me fancying other women now that you are pregnant, because I read in one of those baby magazines that pregnant woman can get paranoid about such things?"

"No Nick" I laughed "I'm not getting paranoid I was just thinking about how pretty she is, surely she must be with someone?"

Nick looked thoughtful. "I've known Anna for years, she's a very private person, I don't think she's married - but to be honest I'm not sure" he answered.

"Have you ever been to her house?" I asked evenly.

Nick stopped eating and put down his knife and fork.

"What's this about?" Nick suddenly said angrily "no, I've never been to her house, I don't even know where she lives, yes she is extremely beautiful and I know there have been rumours about us over the years, but I've never even thought of her in any romantic way, she not my type, she's way too beautiful for me".

My blood began to boil "oh well, I didn't know there were rumours about you two, well that's very, very interesting, oh and she's way too beautiful for you, so what you are saying then is, your type is me, the unattractive type!"

I pushed my plate violently and watched all the green vegetables slide to the floor.

The next day I found Nora and asked her to meet me at lunchtime. At first, she was a bit off with me but then she agreed. I invited Trisha too and the three of us went to the same restaurant that Trisha and I had gone to before. As soon as we sat down, Trisha said to Nora "I told her about Anna".

Nora said, "well, it's about time she knew the truth"

Trisha said eagerly, "tell her about your investigations".

Nora looked around furtively as she lowered her voice and said:

"As soon as Trisha told me what she'd seen I started to ask around about Anna, no one seemed to know anything about her, whether she was in a relationship or where she lived or anything. So, one day after work I followed her. I tucked my hair up in a cap and changed into dark jeans and a dark baggy top, so I looked like a boy. I waited outside across the road for ages but she didn't leave the office. After a couple of hours as it started to get dark, I got fed up and was going to go home but then I saw her leaving the building. She walked for what seemed like ages into the forest and into this creek and as I looked down, there were crabs around my feet. Luckily, I was wearing heavy boots. I got scared and wanted to turn back but something made me keep walking. I was worried in case she turned around and saw me, but she never did. Then out of nowhere I saw a little wooden hut and Anna went inside and I heard an old man's voice say, "Come here my darling, Soucan". I was so scared, I tiptoed quietly out of the forest. I thought they would find me, I kept turning around to check and I kept tripping up, but luckily, I got out alive and I'm here to tell the tale. But I don't tell anyone about it anymore because no-one believes me".

Nora sighed and looked around again lowering her voice even further, "and that's when Trisha and I figured it out for sure, it's confirmed in her name ANNA SOUCAN. Turn it around and say it fast SOUCAN ANNA it's SOUCANYANT- she is a She-Devil!"

I gasped in horror. "Oh my God, does Nick know?" I asked.

"We thought about telling him" said Trisha "but he's so in awe of her he'd never believe us, so we kept it to ourselves. In fact, every man is in awe of her, I mean she's sex on legs!"

We all sat silent for a minute and then I asked, "did you ever hear rumours about Nick and Anna?"

Nora and Trisha exchanged glances at each other but neither spoke.

"What is it?" I demanded.

Neither of them spoke. I felt sick to my stomach "please tell me" I pleaded.

Nora nodded at Trisha and Trisha looked at me and said, "if we tell you, you must promise to keep it to yourself, you must never tell anyone".

"I promise" I whispered.

"Well" said Trisha "there was this old bloke called Bert he used to be the security guard at the office a while back. He said that one night he heard a noise from upstairs in the office and he went up to investigate. It was dark, he thought everyone had gone home but then he saw Nick at his desk. He said that, Nick looked like he had fallen asleep, his head was resting on the desk. Anna was standing over him, Bert said she was wearing her cream trousers and high heeled boots but she was completely topless, he said she was so beautiful he'd never seen anyone so lovely. Anyway, he said that Anna was bending over Nick and seemed to be sucking his neck and stroking his hair lovingly. Bert said she had an egg timer on the desk and every few minutes she would look up to check the egg timer, before sucking Nick's neck again. Bert said it went on like that with Anna checking the egg timer and sucking Nick's blood for about six minutes. Bert said every time Anna stood up to check the egg timer, her breasts were displayed for his full view and they were heavy and soft looking and it reminded him of the fleshiest juiciest mangoes. Apparently, Bert said he got so distracted and a bit excited, that he made a sound and Anna looked up and saw him. He said her face twisted into an evil scowl and she cried out "get out, get out!"

Nora carried on where Trisha had broken off:

"The next day, Nick called into work sick and he didn't come back for over a week. When he returned he looked quite drained. We don't think he knew anything about what had happened. Bert came back to work the next day and just had time to tell his colleague, what he'd seen. Then Anna called Bert to her office, there was some shouting and Bert left the building very distraught looking. They say on the way home he fell over and rolled into a ditch, when he was found he was dead. His body had been pecked to bits by a flock of crows".

"It was probably Anna" Trisha sighed "she turned herself into a crow and pecked him to death".

"God" I said, "I wonder what all that egg-timer stuff was about, it doesn't make sense".

"Well that's what we thought but then I did some research" said Nora "and apparently if a vampire sucks a human's blood for more than six and a half minutes then the human will die because after that the blood loss would be too great, too much vital fluids drained and the heart rate would change, resulting in death".

"But why would she spare Nick's life?" I said in hushed tones.

"Well" Nora sighed "we think perhaps Nick is the mortal she most loves. But we are not sure if she can love because there is darkness in her, where she should have a soul".

Chapter 23

The next day I found it difficult to look at Anna, without imagining her as an evil old hag, sucking the blood out of my Nick's neck. There was also something about the way she laughed and touched Nick when she spoke that irritated me, she'd always been like that around him, but now it seemed so obvious, like someone had just turned on the light and I could at last see clearly. She twirled her hair and pouted her lips, swaying her wide hips as she walked back to her office. I recoiled as I could see the outline of her lacy panties, through her very tight trousers. I looked at her feet, I wanted to see her cloven foot, but she always wore pointy patent high heeled boots.

The day before the twelve-week scan, Nick was ecstatic, he played Beethoven on repeat and hummed along like a busy bee. We took the afternoon off work to attend the appointment. The scan confirmed the pregnancy and Nick's eyes glazed over in awe when we saw the baby move and heard the strong heartbeat. I was relieved as I had begun to feel quite sick and tired in recent days but I now put that down to the shock of finding out about Anna. Christmas was approaching and I vowed to enjoy my pregnancy and my life with Nick and not to worry about all the business with Anna.

When we got home we cuddled up together and Nick suggested that we start to think of baby names, he suggested a few names for boys and girls. I was thoughtful and then I said, "would you mind if we called the baby Toby if it's a boy?" Nick cuddled me tight. "Of course, I don't mind that's an excellent idea"

Nick said. I thought of Toby in his Spider-Man bathing pants years before and I smiled deeply with satisfaction.

A few days later I had a niggling back pain and my wee was stingy when I went to the toilet. Nick called the doctor straight away and they said it sounded like I had a urine infection, he made an appointment for the next day. But that night the pain got worse. Nick was sound asleep so I didn't wake him. I paced up and down but I was worried that the urine infection would affect the baby. The next day a urine infection was confirmed, I was given anti-biotics to take and had to drink plenty of fluids to flush the infection out of my system. Nick went back to work but insisted that I stayed at home to rest while I was on the anti-biotics. I was so thankful that it was just a urine infection, that I thanked God constantly in my head. After a week I returned to work, Anna invited me to her office and welcomed me back. I tried my best not to make too much eye contact with her deep penetrating eyes, but it was impossible.

A few days later I woke up and felt different, my back no longer had pain and my breasts were no longer tender. I went to the toilet and there was a little bleeding but no pain. I told Nick, I could see worry cross his face, but he said bleeding during early pregnancy was normal. "But I'm thirteen weeks pregnant" I sobbed.

"Don't think the worst Connie, let's go to the hospital" Nick said shakily.

At the hospital the nurse did a pregnancy test, she smiled brightly and said it had come back positive. Nick and I gasped a sign of relief and cried some happy tears. We got up to go home but then a doctor came out and said they needed to do some more tests. I was prodded and poked and examined by ultra sound. We were asked to wait in a small waiting room, where we nervously held hands. After a few minutes we were called into an office with the doctor. I knew straight away it was bad news. The doctor cleared his throat and said "I'm afraid you are most certainly having a miscarriage".

Nick gasped out loud "that can't be right! The nurse said that the pregnancy test we just did was positive, surely it's just a urine infection?" Nick sounded desperate, I couldn't bear to look at him.

The doctor looked at Nick and then at me his eyes seemed kind. "Unfortunately these tests are not always accurate because it can take up to nine weeks for the pregnancy hormone HCG to leave the system after a miscarriage... But I'm afraid there is further sad news".

Nick and I exchanged nervous glances and looked at the doctor again. The doctor sympathetically explained that my previous abortion had been done very badly and part of my cervix and fallopian tubes had been damaged. He said it was a miracle that I'd got pregnant at all but without a doubt I would never be able to carry a baby to full term. He said there was nothing that could be done, other than let nature run its course. He prescribed some pain killers.

"Oh God, no, please" Nick cried out, tears streaming down his face.

On the way home in the car we said nothing to each other but we both cried silent tears. A few hours later I doubled-over in pain, the pains in my stomach were horrendous. Nick ran to me, he rubbed my back up and down, he held me and we cried out in shocked and agonizing pain, as I passed the products of our conception, the beginnings of what would have been a human life.

The next few days filled me with an overwhelming sense of sadness and fear. All I could do was lay on my bed and cry, life seemed utterly unbearable.

Nick dealt with our loss by becoming really angry - he cleared the fridge of all the healthy food and folic acid tablets. He threw away all the baby books, I even watched in horror as he broke the Beethoven CD in half and chucked it in the bin. He tore out all the pages in my baby journal and burnt them.

After a few days, Nick said "you can't hide in your bed forever, we both need to pull ourselves together and face going into work".

A week later I had to go back for a scan to make sure the miscarriage was complete. Nick took me to the appointment. In the car on the way we were silent but then out of the blue Nick said angrily "you never told me you had an abortion before!" I ignored him, I didn't answer, I turned my head away in an attempt to hide the tears streaming down my face. When we got to the hospital, he looked a bit hurt and confused when I asked him not to stay with me. His angry response to our loss was making me resent him, unselfishness had in the past come naturally to him, but now I was seeing another side of him I didn't like.

I told him I would make my own way back and promised to get a taxi home. I watched him drive away, he was broken.

I went through the ultrasound procedure in a numb

daze as I looked at the black emptiness on the screen. No baby, confirmed. No heartbeat, confirmed.

I walked out of the hospital in a blaze of blinding sunlight. I needed to get a taxi home but I didn't want to go home. I didn't know where to turn, I walked about aimlessly until I came to a busy walled square, it was teeming with people waiting at a bus stop and taxi rank. I realised at once where I was and I sat on the wall and watched the white house standing tall and proud in the landscape. I looked around for the old man and wondered if I had imagined him and his crooked half smile.

A young teenaged girl sat next to me she was looking down at her hands, I followed her gaze and recognised the printed card in her hand it said **Ms C La Corbel- Clairvoyant and Midwifery Services.**

Then an older girl approached, she snatched the card out of the younger girl's hand, "don't even think about it" the older girl shouted "that woman is a Churile".

I remembered Gran telling us about a Churile, what did she say? I couldn't remember. I walked to the library, I looked it up. It said:

A Churile is the spirit of a pregnant woman who committed suicide during pregnancy. A Churile is in eternal grief since she lost her child. A Churile's victim is a pregnant woman, who she follows and possesses out of envy. Her attacks on women take the form of miscarriages.

I walked out of the library in dismay, Christmas was approaching and all I could feel was fear for the future and disappointment. A few weeks before I was excited and hopeful and full of optimism. Now I was filled with a black hole of sorrow and it was all my fault for going to a Churile in the first place. If only I had told Michael I was pregnant, he would have married me and we would have had a couple of children by now. I messed everything up.

I looked around me and noticed mothers with their cute little children all about the square, I wanted to scream and scream with despair.

When I got home it was dark and late. I saw Nick sitting slumped in a chair, his head in his hands. He looked up as I walked in, "where were you, I was worried" he said sadly.

"I just needed some space" I answered.

"I was thinking" said Nick a note of hope creeping into his voice "we could always adopt a child".

"No, Nick" I sighed "we need to grieve properly for this loss first, before we start rushing into adoption".

Nick looked straight at me, a light went out in his eyes, his face collapsed inwards, he looked like a little boy who had been let down, hurt and innocent with his sad puppy dog eyes. His shoulders slumped and he bent his head down again and collapsed into tears.

"I'm going to have a bath" I said and walked away.

I ran the bath and submerged myself in soothing bubbles, I began to relax when suddenly I started crying harder than I'd ever cried in my life before.

Chapter 24

Going back to work was difficult, everyone was kind to me but it was awkward no-one knew quite what to say. Nick and I barely spoke anymore in the office or at home. I wondered if everyone in the office noticed our strained relationship. Nick's presence made the reality of the miscarriage smack home, I wanted him to disappear. Christmas was approaching and the air was filled with festive cheer, except Nick and I were on the outskirts looking in, like uninvited guests.

Nora and Trisha were nice to me, but Nora had now found out, she too was pregnant and her and Trisha were often talking about babies and pregnancy. They tried to be discreet around me, but their voices were loud even in whispers and each conversation about babies, was like a dagger in my heart.

To make matters worse, Trisha had now started to show, she had a round neat belly and she walked like a pregnant woman, and had 'the glow'.

After a scan she came back to the office and her and Nora gazed adoringly at the scan picture of her unborn baby. I saw Nick looking at them, he smiled at Trisha and congratulated her, but he could not conceal the pain on his face. Then Anna came out of her office, she asked to see the picture, I could see fear in Trisha's eyes as she hesitatingly handed the scan picture to Anna. Anna studied the scan photo, then she handed it back and smiled and said "nice, now get back to work and stop chatting!"

At lunchtime a few days later, Nora said she had concocted a plan to expose Anna as a soucanyant. She said that her great grandma had said, that the young skin that the soucanyant wears over her old skin can be destroyed with salt. Nora's plan was that at the Christmas party, the three of us would all coat our hands in salt and then shake Anna's hand in turn and that should be enough salt to melt away some of her new skin and expose her old lady skin underneath.

"Oh, and I would love to expose her cloven foot" I said excitedly. "Yes" said Nora "I can pretend to get dizzy due to my pregnancy and then I could spill my drink all over her foot and then she'd have to take her boots off".

"That's an excellent idea" laughed Trisha.

Over the next few days we perfected our plan. I felt excited, Nick noticed and commented "you seem a bit perked up, Connie"

Yes, I smiled "I'm just looking forward to the office Christmas party".

"It should be a good night" Nick answered; the caterers are top notch and the DJ is well known. It's taking place poolside too, so it should be fun and oh, Anna invited Dad as well, to thank him for sending some good contacts the company's way".

Nick's Dad! Oh, how awkward would that be! I smiled a false smile "that sounds lovely" I answered.

The night of the party I was taking no chances, I moisturised my hands, then I put as much salt on top as I could, to make sure it stuck. Just to be sure I slipped a plastic container of salt in my handbag.

The venue was spectacular, all the trees at the side of the pool were dressed in white fairy lights from the trunk of the trees, to the tops of their branches. The band was playing parang music and the ambiance filled me with a sense of future happiness. I held Nick's hand, as we entered, he seemed surprised but pleased.

As we walked in I saw Trisha and Nora waiting for me near the Christmas tree. I ran over to them excitedly, leaving Nick to catch up with a couple of the office boys. The Christmas tree was large and beautifully dressed. Nora said it was modelled on the Christmas tree at the Rockefeller centre in New York.

"Are you ready girls?" I giggled. "I've brought some more salt so we can top up in the bathroom if you want".

The three of us ran to the bathroom giggling in our impossibly high heels, we added a good dose of salt to our hands, then Nora said "let's go and expose that bitch girls" we giggled like naughty school children.

Anna was standing near the band, she was surrounded by a group of men all gawping at her. She looked radiant in a black tight fitting long maxi dress that hugged her curves. She looked like a sexual goddess with her shiny black hair and pouty red lips. She had just the right amount of cleavage showing, to tantalize and tease.

The three of us walked over to her, our salted hands outstretched. I smiled sweetly. "Oh Anna you look lovely". I stretched out my hand to shake hers, she twirled her hair, she smiled back , she held out her hand but before I knew what was happening Nick's father's large frame filled my view, he took my hand and shook it firmly, then he pulled me towards him and slapped me on the bum. "Wow, Connie" he beamed in his loud voice, "you look well, and look at these beauties behind you" and he looked lecherously at Nora and Trisha shaking their hands vigorously in turn.

Nick's father suddenly looked confused, he looked down at his hand it was covered in bits of salt. He looked up at us and boomed a loud laugh "have you girls coated your hands in salt?"

"Oh yes" said Trisha quickly regaining her composure "salt is very good as a hand exfoliator, it keeps our hands nice and soft" she held up her hands and rubbed them together a bit too enthusiastically.

"I always find exfoliating BEFORE a party is a better method" said Anna in a voice of pure disgust.

The drinks waiter then appeared and Nick's Dad handed out drinks as though he were the host. Suddenly Nora swooned, "Oh God, I feel so dizzy" she said holding her head with one hand, then she fell heavily towards Anna, spilling her drink all over Anna's boots and the bottom of her dress.

"She's pregnant" shouted Trisha and a couple of the young boys carried Nora away and placed her in a chair nearby.

"Oh dear" I said to Anna, "your dress and boots are all wet, let me help you take off your boots so you can dry your feet". I bent down quickly lifted up the bottom of Anna's dress and started searching for the zipper on the boots. I was just about to grab the zip, when a large hand pulled me back. I looked up and Nick's Dad had pulled me up to standing. Anna glared at me, a petrified look on her face. Nick's Dad said, "I will help her, Connie". He already had tissues in his hand. "Come and sit down dear" he said as he guided Anna into a chair. As he bent over to wipe her boots, his gaze lingered a bit too long on Anna's ample bosom. Anna noticed, she looked up and smiled smugly at me, she adjusted her dress pulling down so a bit more of her cleavage was on display and she bent over, smiling and twirling her hair provocatively, as Nick's Dad wiped her boots dry.

Later in the evening Nora, Trisha and I regrouped.

"Well, we failed spectacularly" Trisha sighed.

"She's too clever for us" I said.

"Well, she will always outsmart us because she has the luck of the devil on her side" Nora shrugged.

But later in the night I saw my chance. Anna was standing at the edge of the pool, talking to Nick and Nick's Dad. She was laughing flirtatiously, twirling her hair. I saw red, I needed to expose her cloven foot, to show the world that she was a She-Devil. I grabbed a tray of drinks from a waiter and quickly walked over to Anna and pushed the tray into her. I watched in slow motion, as Anna wobbled and toppled over into the pool. There was a loud gasp from the crowd, I saw Anna floating face down, her black hair fanning out. As quick as a flash Nick and his father dived in, both held Anna under each arm. They dragged her out of the pool and she spluttered out water as she held tightly on to Nick. She was soaked right through and I grinned, now she would have to take off her boots, at last her cloven foot would be exposed.

Nick stared at me a look of horror on his face, I realised I was still grinning and I immediately adjusted my face and tried to look concerned. I ran over and said "oh gosh, let me help". Nick glared at me. A large hand pulled me away again, it was Nick's Dad "I think you have done quite enough!" he said abruptly.

The hotel manager ran over to Anna, he offered her the use of a bedroom and a robe and slippers to change into.

"That's very kind of you" she said in her smooth voice "but I feel a bit out of sorts now and I just want to go home" she reached up and touched Nick's face. "Would you mind driving me home, Nick" she smiled.

Was it possible that she looked more beautiful in her wet

and dishevelled state. Her dress clung to her even more tightly showing off her Marilyn Monroe figure and her hair was swept back from her face wet and straight revealing more of her sculptured face. My plan had failed again, instead of exposing her cloven foot, I had transformed her into a seductive mermaid.

A big wet hand was on my shoulder again, it was Nick's Dad, "come on Connie I will drive you home" he said as he pulled me towards the exit.

Chapter 25

At home the next day, I tried to avoid Nick for as long as possible, I stayed in bed for a long time, but as soon I emerged from the bedroom, Nick was ready for me with questions.

"Well, explain yourself" he shouted.

"Explain what" I said innocently

"Don't play the innocent with me" he shouted again the veins on his head were visible "you pushed Anna in the pool on purpose everyone saw you do it. Dad thinks you are mentally unstable. Mum is worried for me, she doesn't think it's safe for me to live with you anymore!"

I was scared, was Nick going to leave me.

"Please Nick" I said, "you don't understand Anna isn't who you think she is, look I know this sounds strange but we have proof that she's a soucanyant".

"A soucanyant! What the hell is that" Nick sighed.

"She is a She-Devil, Nick" I whispered.

"She-Devil, a She-Devil" Nick laughed "Connie, have you heard yourself? Oh my God, Mum and Dad are right you need serious help".

I sat down heavily I felt exhausted. "Listen Nick do you remember a few years ago when you got really ill and had to take time off work?"

"Yeah, what about it, Connie I hadn't even met you then" Nick said sitting down.

"Well you were ill because Anna had sucked blood from your neck and drained you" I said as calmly as I could.

"Connie" Nick said, standing up again "Connie I was really ill with Dengue fever I had to be hospitalised, I don't know what you are going on about and if she sucked my blood like a vampire why am I still alive?!" Nick sighed and sat down again.

"She only sucked your blood for six minutes - that's why you didn't die"

"Six minutes, as long as that right?" Nick fell about in fits of laughter.

"She lives in the forest, she's really an old hag, in new skin, you need to be careful of her, she's evil" I screamed.

"Connie" Nick said still laughing "she lives in a smart little apartment in Westmoorings, I took her home last night, she doesn't live in a forest".

"Nick listen to me soucanyants feed on the foetuses of unborn babies, she probably sucked all the blood from our baby - that's why it died". I slumped in the chair, I could feel myself sinking into the depths of despair. I knew I was sounding crazy, but I had to get him to believe me.

Nick looked at me, he came over to me and held me in his arms, he smoothed my hair, while I cried.

After I had spent all my tears, I kissed Nick on his cheek, I felt safe in his arms. I looked at him and said, "I love you, Nick".

Nick cupped my face in his hands, he looked in my eyes, his eyes looked painfully sad. "You are not well, Connie" he said slowly "you need professional help".

On Monday morning, Anna called me into her office. She said she had taken witness statements and everyone confirmed that I had pushed her into the pool on purpose. She said that Nick had begged for me, to be given a second chance. She said she had carefully considered Nick's request, but on balance she found my behaviour was totally unacceptable. It was gross misconduct and I was sacked.

Nick's parents set me up to see a top psychiatrist, I was appalled.

"I'm not going Nick" I screamed at him, "I'm not mad".

I mooched about at home unemployed, bored and feeling sorry for myself. I spent large parts of the day in bed. One evening I woke up to hushed voices. I opened the bedroom door quietly and padded in bare feet, so I could hear more clearly. In the mirror I could see Nick and Anna in the living room.

Nick looked distraught "I don't know what to do" he sniffed "she's always talked about her family being cursed and crows and black magic but this is something on another scale, she seems to think you are the devil incarnate".

Anna put her hand on Nick's knee, "I'm so sorry" she said in her smooth voice "losing the baby has obviously pushed her over the edge" she sighed.

Nick put his hand over Anna's hand on his knee, "it's so cruel" he said shaking his head "God gave us a tantalising glimpse of something amazing but then he snatched it away!"

Anna rose to her feet, she touched Nick's shoulder, "maybe give her some space" she said, "but you know where I am if you need me".

I padded quietly back to the bedroom and lay on the bed, listening to the sound of Anna's car driving away.

A few weeks later Nick came home with a large suitcase. I watched as he began angrily shoving his clothes into it.

"What are you doing" I said in shocked surprise.

"I'm leaving you" Nick said as tears appeared at the corners of his eyes.

I stood looking at him packing, I was numb I couldn't speak.

"I'm sorry" he said" I can't do this anymore, we are both young enough to start again and meet new people, this isn't working between us, you must know that. I've tried to help you Connie, but you won't help yourself".

"But, Nick" I said my voice croaking "maybe we could go to counselling together, maybe we could consider adopting! Please, Nick" I began to sob, "please don't go".

Nick paused and looked at me, "if I stay it would be out of pity for you, not love, I don't love you the way I used too, your crazy behaviour, has turned my love into concern and pity". Nick paused again and continued "I'm sorry to say this, Connie, but I have a deep yearning to be a father and I don't think adoption could fulfil that need".

"Well, that tells me" I said abruptly.

"Look, Connie, you can keep the apartment and the company car. I will send you an allowance every month, so you will be ok".

"So, you have it all figured out then", I smirked bitterly.

Nick looked around making sure he hadn't forgotten anything, then he turned to me and said calmly "by the way, Anna was born with club feet, not cloven feet".

"Oh yes how do you know?! Did you see her club feet when you were getting naked with her?" I screeched.

Nick stared at me, he shook his head in a pitying way, he approached me and kissed me on the top of my head. "Have a good life and look after yourself" he smiled at me.

He picked up his suitcase and turned towards the door.

"Go on then walk away, you fucking bastard" I heard myself shout.

I watched him walk slowly out of the apartment and out of my life forever.

Chapter 26

So, I found myself all alone. For weeks I had no contact with people, with no work, marriage and the loss of loved ones around, I was in my own silent private world. At first, I found the solitude comforting, I could think, breathe freely, read and rest without being disturbed, my heart was my own again. But after a while I began to feel isolated and lonely. I had too much time to think about the past and all the negative and horrible events in my life.

For some reason I found myself pining for an old love, but strangely enough I wasn't pining for Nick, but for Michael. I realised that Michael was really my one true love, I had never loved Nick the way I loved Michael. I had fallen madly head over heels for Michael, I had been besotted with him and I couldn't get him out of my head. I longed to be near him and found myself dreaming about him every night, replaying our nights of passion.

I hadn't seen Michael for quite a few years but I decided that I needed to see him again, to see if getting back with him was a possibility. Every day I woke up and I decided that this would be the day to go to see him but I always got scared and abandoned my plans.

One day I took a call from Trisha, she had given birth to a healthy baby boy and invited me to the christening. As she ended the call she said "Connie, I'd like you to come to the christening but it may be difficult, because Nick and Anna are now an item and they are very lovey dovey together".

The next day I resolved to see Michael, I woke up early carefully styling my hair and applying my make-up with lashings of mascara and red lipstick. I carefully chose a tight-fitting dress that stopped just above my knees and high heels, black shiny shoe-boots. I had a matching handbag. I looked in the mirror and was pleased, I looked smoking hot.

I went to Michael's garage, I saw him straight away, hunched over the bonnet of a car with two younger lads in overalls besides him. I posed at the door of the garage, with one hand on my hip, I tilted my head like a model. One of the young lads looked up, he took a double take and wolf whistled at me. Michael turned around, he looked at me, a broad smile swept across his face and he approached me. Happiness filled me as he approached, I realised that he was the most handsome and intriguing looking man I had ever seen.

"Wow, Connie", he said in this deep gruff voice, "you look great, but what are you doing here, do you have car problems?"

"No" I giggled tossing my hair, "I was just in the area and thought I'd say hello".

"Well that's nice, do you want to grab a coffee in the café around the corner?" he grinned.

As we sat in the café over our cups of coffee, I noticed that his broad shoulders had thickened with even more muscle and his skin seemed more coarse and tanned. His hair was shorter in small tight neat curls. He looked good and pleasure welled up inside of me. I had an overwhelming desire to tell him how I felt. It was now or never. I began rubbing my ear and smiling provocatively.

"Michael", I said, "I have been thinking of you a lot recently, my love and desire for you and all the passion we shared has recently just risen up in me and taken me by surprise and I realise now that you are my one true love. No-one else will ever come close. Michael you are the one".

The smile on Michael's face drained away and then he laughed a short humourless laugh "this is a joke right?" he said looking at me his eyes squinting.

I looked at his handsome face and I knew I was no longer responsible for my actions, I grabbed his oil stained hand and said softly "Michael I love you deeply I always have and always will, let's try again, we owe it to ourselves to be happy".

Michael looked at my hand over his, a look of repulsion crossed his face and he abruptly pulled his hand away.

"Are you serious, Connie? I thought you were married", he choked over his coffee.

"Yes of course I'm serious. My marriage failed, Michael, because I was still in love with you, I'm still in love with you now. Let's get back together. Please let's just give it one more try". I answered, a note of pleading creeping in.

Michael looked around the café, he shook his head in disbelief. "Connie we broke up years ago, and do you remember it was me that broke it off with you. I broke up with you because we were not on the same page, yes it was good between us at first but then it became obvious, we were not compatible. You thought you were too good for the likes of a greasy mechanic like me, you looked down on me and my parents. My Mamma didn't like you and she likes everyone and even my Dad thought your head was stuck up your own arse. Sorry to be rude Connie, but did you think I would be waiting around for you for years, on the off chance that you may have developed a better personality".

I gulped back tears, hurt and pride. "But Michael, you said you'd always love me, you wrote me that poem remember?"

Michael seemed speechless. I remembered how Michael had dumped me the first time and now I had given him the power to dump me all over again.

Michael looked at me sympathetically. "Look Connie, you are still fairly attractive, I'm sure you could find someone to love you, I'm sure you are just on the rebound from the breakup of your marriage" he said still shaking his head in a sort of disbelief.

A piercing hurt stabbed me in the chest, did he just call me 'fairly attractive'? I'd made my best effort to look exceptionally beautiful and sexy and he just dealt me a low blow and insulted me by saying I was still fairly attractive!

I blinked trying to compose myself, fighting back any sign of agony or emotion.

Michael continued "anyway I'm in a committed and loving relationship and I have eighteen-month-old twin boys. I'm desperately and hopelessly in love with my boys and my girlfriend. My parents love my girlfriend to bits. She's down to earth and genuine and she doesn't think she's better than them. In fact, I think you know her, you know her well".

My brain started to spin "I know your girlfriend?" I asked in a sort of whisper.

"Yes" Michael smiled, he was so attractive it pained me. "Yes, the love of my life is your good friend Martha Grainger" he said.

"Martha" I gasped.

"Yes", Michael replied "I didn't know you two knew each other when we first met, but then she started to speak about you when you were getting married and I realised you were the same Connie that I knew but I didn't say anything to Martha, because you obviously didn't tell her about us, so I thought what she doesn't know can't hurt her. I know you don't keep in touch with Martha that often anymore, but if you want to stay friends with her that's fine by me. She has her own business now, you could visit her there. But obviously in view of your feelings for me, I suggest you keep your distance from me, after today, to avoid any awkwardness or uncertainty".

"Martha" I gasped in a whisper again to myself.

Michael called the waiter over and paid the bill, then he got up from the table and put his hand on my shoulder and said "look after yourself, Connie. I do hope you find what you are looking for, but you need to know it's not me!" I watched him walk out of the café, tall, handsome and proud.

I sat in a daze, at the little wooden table, in the busy café, lonelier than ever before. I thought about Martha, she had achieved her perfect life and I was the tragic, second best victim of unrequited love.

Chapter 27

The episode with Michael left me embarrassed and hollow. The humiliation rose up to meet me every morning as I opened my eyes. I imagined Martha and her twin boys with her gorgeous Michael and her bachelor's degree in media and fashion. She had achieved all that I hadn't, the love of a good man, children, a university degree and a career. A perfect life.

A few months later I thought of Mum, I hadn't seen her for some time but I had heard that she had moved in with her new boyfriend and had settled down. I kept putting off visiting her but I suddenly decided to bite the bullet and do my duty as a good Catholic daughter. It was nearly Christmas time again, another year had past and a visit to her was long overdue. I called and told her I would visit her on Sunday, she sounded really excited and said she would cook for me. As I drove the long drive back to the south of the island, memories of the old life I'd left behind began to haunt me, I felt a deep dread in the pit off my stomach and I had to fight the compulsion to turn back.

The house was at the end of a dirt track road and it was more of a large wooden hut rather than a house. But there was something charming about it as it stood enveloped by large coconut trees and the cloudless blue sky. As soon as I pulled up, I could see Mum rush out onto the veranda. She looked tiny, much more petite than I remembered. Next to her was a tall straight white man, with a mop of grey hair. As I approached, Mum rushed towards me hugged me and said, "hello darling, come meet Mr Alberto, my partner". Mr Alberto extended his hand towards me and shook my hand with vigour. He had deep blue eyes, marred by deep wrinkles around them, his eyes were kindly and his smile was warm. "Welcome Constance" he said "your Mum has told me so much about you, it's so nice to meet you at last... you want a sweet drink or a coconut water or something stronger?" I explained that I was driving and a coconut water would be fine. I squirmed at the thought of a sweet drink, I would never ruin my perfect figure with a sweet drink. Mum led me by the hand into the house, I could see in her eyes she was proud of it. Despite the wooden exterior, the interior was bright and airy. The dual aspect windows gave a great unspoilt view of undulating green hills.

There was a beautiful carved wooden bureau at one end of the room and another beautifully crafted display cabinet at another end. At the heart of the room was a small round oak dining table with queen anne legs, high back chairs which also had queen anne legs. Apart from that the room was bare, save for two well-worn leather wing chairs which would not have looked out of place in a stately home.

"You like it" Mum said with real pride in her voice, "Mr Alberto is a furniture restorer and carpenter" she chirped. I made you curry goat and dal pouri, come sit down, I will dish it out for you. You look skinny girl like you don't eat!"

As Mum busied herself in the kitchen, I looked into the display cabinet and saw that Mum had a selection of framed pictures. One seemed recent of Ben and his family. The others were older of Ben, Toby and I from when we were little, some with Mum and Dad. Happy smiling photos of a past life, in beautifully carved frames. I felt a pang of sadness wrench the pit of my stomach and I quickly looked away before the tears welled up in my eyes.

The curried goat was peppery and delicious and the dal pouri was soft and paper thin. Mum had always been a good cook. We chatted easily just like old times and she told me that she had got a job in the oil factory as a cleaner which would give her a little pension and Mr Alberto was getting a lot of work as a cabinet maker from the big oil company directors and through word of mouth the work was pouring in. She said she was happy, she had stopped drinking, except for very occasionally. She said Mr Alberto was a good man and was looking after her.

As she spoke I felt a deep sense of sorrow for my mother, she had been a beautiful woman with such high prospects. Before Dad died, she had had brilliant jobs as executive personal assistant's to many a company director, of the biggest firms in Trinidad. Her looks meant she could have commanded the attention of any man. Here she was now, a shell of the woman she once was, her back was stooped, her skin was darkened and leathered by too much exposure to the sun and she had lost a couple of her front teeth. Here she was, settling for life as a cleaner with a man twice her age. My poor mother, my heart bled for her, but at least in her own way she was happy. As we spoke, I could see Mr Alberto in the yard playing with two large Alsatian dogs and on reflection I could see, after all she'd been through, how she could settle for this simple life.

After a few pleasant hours as I was preparing to leave, Mr Alberto came through the back door and I politely remarked "Mr Alberto the furniture you have made is lovely, you are very skilled". Mr Alberto looked pleased but what he said next shocked me.

"Yes, I have a skill but thanks to your brother Ben I have been able to turn my skill into a real living, your brother is a real godsend".

Mum coughed uncomfortably and shifted uneasily on her feet, she said:

"Yes your brother Ben has been sending us $500 a month and it has really helped us. Mr Alberto has been able to buy good quality wood and antiques to restore and we manage to put a bit aside each month for a rainy day".

My mouth felt dry and I felt my face flush hot, as guilt consumed me. My voice came out in a croak. "Oh Mum, I'm sorry" I said "I could have sent you money too if you asked".

As soon as I said the words I knew instinctively that Ben would not have asked and that he would have just realised that Mum would benefit from extra money. He sent the money without asking, knowing that Mum was too proud to ask us for anything. Deep down for all his protestations and denial of his Catholic faith, Ben was the one who was the good Catholic child, honouring his mother, no matter what her faults. I felt totally ashamed.

Mum looked uneasy and she grabbed me and hugged me tight. Mum looked me in the eye and said in a kind voice "don't feel guilty Constance we don't expect anything from you, we know you've had a hard life, with your marriage failing and everything and Oh God, we heard you are barren!"

Mr Alberto sighed heavily, "being barren must be the hardest thing for a young woman like you, we know you have your own troubles and besides your brother is a big shot lawyer in England, he can afford it. He sending tickets for we to visit him and his family in England in the summer holidays, so his kids can spend time with their grandmother".

At this Mum beamed, no longer able to conceal her glee to spare my feelings, her smile lit up her whole face. "He says he going to take us to see Buckingham Palace and Hampton court, we really excited, I never even been on a plane before" Mum added and as she said this her eyes sparkled with excitement.

On the way home I felt physically sick, my head felt like it had expanded into a heavy burden, the pit of my stomach felt empty.

Ben, Ben, Ben! the stupid little dunce boy, who never went to church, who never went to school, who never did anything he was supposed to, how did he become the perfect son, the perfect big shot lawyer, with his perfect beautiful wife and his perfect nuclear family, with his two children a boy and a girl, for good measure!

I was the one who was meant to have the perfect life. I made a pact with Martha! What went so wrong... where is my perfect life! My head expanded with a heavy green jealous rage!

As I drove around the Savannah in Port of Spain, I saw a couple holding hands and laughing. The woman looked familiar. She had long dark wavy hair and she was heavily pregnant. I strained my neck to get a better view and realised, as I'd thought, it was Nick and Anna. Nick was no longer the skinny beanpole I'd married, he had put on some weight and looked content. A scream came out of my mouth filling the car with a deafening sound.

I don't even know how I got home, I must have been on automatic pilot. As soon as I got through my front door, I slid down to the floor and burst into tears. I thought of the smiling pictures in Mum's cabinet, the happy family days. Then my thoughts turned to Dad dying, the bad times with Mum, the time with Granny, Bandit hanging, Toby's accident and the Corbeau, Michael, my babies stolen away by a Churile, Anna a soucanyant how could she be pregnant and everything began to whirl in my head.

The next day I woke up with a banging headache, I was lying on the floor, still by my front door. Suddenly a word sprung to mind "barren" they called me "barren" my womb is "barren". I had heard the term used like that before, for women who could not have children, but I never thought of myself as barren. The word was ugly and cruel. How dare they call me barren, what an awful, hurtful word. Suddenly I rushed to the bookcase and grabbed the oxford dictionary leafing through the pages until I found the word: Barren - 1st meaning – 'unproductive, infertile, unfruitful, arid, desert, waste, desolate' 2nd meaning – 'showing no results or achievements, unproductive'.

I felt gutted, robbed of all emotion, I pondered the meaning of the word and of my life. So that's how I was viewed, not as Constance the success with a perfect life, but as Constance the poor thing, with her broken marriage, her broken life and her barren womb. I could suddenly see the irony of my situation, my life was anything but perfect. Even my mother with her wooden hut and her cleaning job, had more than me. My life was barren! I suddenly felt the urge to laugh, it was all so comical. A big belly laugh caught me by surprise, I was suddenly in fits of hysterics, I began spinning around and laughing as though I were being tickled, I suddenly shouted out "I'm a waste, I'm a desert nothing can grow in me", I giggled and giggled and gigged, until I felt dizzy and totally drained.

I must have dozed off and when I woke and my eyes refocused, I looked around my posh minimalist apartment. I had thought it beautiful with its clean lines and sparse objects. Now I saw it in a new light. This apartment is sterile, it is barren I thought.

I suddenly heard whispering voices, they were sniggering and laughing behind my back. "You are barren" they were whispering "barren, barren, barren" they laughed "you are sterile, you can't bear fruit. Ben is the chosen angel, he is a success, you are a failure, you will be caste out to live with the unclean spirits. One voice shouted louder than the rest it said "you is a damn disgrace, you can't even help your own mother".

I turned around and I could see the vapour of the voices coming from the plug sockets. All of a sudden my thoughts became clear and I felt calm. I knew then what I had to do, the solution had been there all along, I can't think why I didn't realise it before. It was so obvious now when I think of it... I had to get the strongest masking tape to block up the plug sockets, to keep my mind clear.

Chapter 28

After I had blocked up all the plug sockets, I thought that I would feel calm but that night I slept fitfully. I felt myself being transported back to Michael's annex. The annex was enclosed by shards of light. I peered through the window and I could see Michael standing with his back to me. His tight buttocks and ripped muscles, glistened in the sunlight, he was totally naked. My heart strings tugged as I recalled his beautiful golden tanned body and all at once I longed for him to turn around and wrap me up in his taut strong arms. His hair was still long and curly and brushed against his broad shoulders.

Michael seemed to be speaking to someone and when he moved aside I could see Anna sitting on his bed. I gasped as I saw that she too was naked. Her long black hair hung loosely down to her waist. Her lips were red, her black eyes sparkled as she looked up and smiled lovingly at Michael. My heart pulled at my sadness. Her skin was smooth and silk like, her breasts which were fully exposed hung pendulous and voluptuous. Her areolas were large and almost black and yet her nipples were pink and protruded out unnaturally long. The sight of her a pure carnal woman, gave her a sensual desirability which took my breath away but made me loathe her. I could see why Michael wouldn't be able to resist her. Michael turned towards her, his penis was erect and it seemed grotesquely enlarged, it was a purple pink colour and was visibly throbbing.

Anna raised her slender arms and took his penis in her hands; her talons were painted a bright red to match her lips. She bent her head and kissed his erection, when she raised her head again I could see that she had left the shape of her lips in lipstick upon his still throbbing member.

The pain in my heart surged forward into rage. The scene I witnessed seemed to represent an ultimate almost sacred love. I banged on the window wildly, I shouted in between sobs at Anna "leave him alone, that is *my* Michael, *my* Michael - not yours".

They didn't hear me and Michael lovingly took Anna's hand and kissed it.

Somewhere from inside I heard the sounds of a baby crying. Michael turned to the corner of the room where a heavily ornate silver baby's crib stood, he walked a few steps, reached down into the crib and lifted a baby in his arms. He smiled and cooed at the baby, who was wrapped in a soft linen white cloth.

Michael took the baby over to Anna and she stood up to take the baby in her arms. When she stood up her very voluptuous breasts cascaded down in tandem with her black flowing hair. Looking at her beauty and the lovely family scene, of Anna, Michael and their baby, I felt a pang of jealousy twist my heart.

I tried to pull myself away from the window but as I did so, my eye caught something which held my attention. Anna's tummy was smooth as silk but as I looked lower her vagina was covered in a grey unruly mess of hair. I lowered my eyes further and noticed that her legs were thin and wrinkled as though they were the legs of an old woman. Suddenly the baby turned his head at an odd 90-degree angle towards me. He looked like a cute little cherub, he had pink lips and a mass of curly hair. His skin was the colour of golden syrup. As he turned to me, he extended one of his chubby little hands towards me- he smiled at me and said "Mamma".

I realised at once that this child was my baby, mine and Michael's baby. I banged on the window screaming "Michael that is our baby - not hers". Just then all three of them turned to look at me - Anna shifted and I got a full body view of her. One of her feet was wrinkled and old with what looked like yellowed curled toe nails, the other foot was a cow's hoof.

Horrified I turned away as quickly as I could. I tried to run but my feet felt heavy as though I were walking in glue, I stumbled. When I looked up I saw a tree, its branches were bare, mangled and deformed. On one branch a dog was hanging from a lead. It was Bandit, his distinctive black patch around one eye. His eye balls were bulging, fixed and dilated. His mouth hung open, spittle dripping from a pink swollen tongue.

Under the tree Selassi sat, he lit a ganja joint and winked at me. When he turned his head, I could see his dreadlocks had parted to reveal a large bloody gash on the back of his head. On the highest branch of the tree a Raven was devouring its carrion, its black plumage contrasted majestically with the dead flesh in its beak.

I got up and walked away as quickly as I could and then I saw a red car, there was a large dent at the front and the fender was hanging off. Toby lay at the front of the car on the road, in his school uniform. He looked like he was sleeping. A small pocket of blood had collected near the side of his mouth. A large red faced Corbeau with a long white beak and red rimmed black eyes, stood watching Toby.

Then I heard Daddy's voice, he said "Connie, it's not your time, go back home".

Chapter 29

I awoke to bright lights and a hospital bed, it seemed that I had been hospitalised for my own health and safety. I didn't know how time could be lost so quickly but by the time I awoke to the conscious reality of being in a locked ward, I had been there for three weeks.

The doctor said I had to be heavily sedated as I had been very volatile, angry and distressed. I was on Petal Ward, otherwise known as the 'mad ward'. It seemed I had blocked up all the plugs at home, which had caused a fire. The doctor stated that I had to be rescued from the burning flames.

The doctor's eyes reminded me of dark pebbles too close together, framed by thick bushy eye brows. Her breath had the faint whiff of alcohol. Her nose was large and looked like a beak. She had black, coarse, unruly hair. I looked at her and pitied her, as she spoke to me and took notes.

She asked me why I blocked up the plugs at home. I paused for a long time, I considered keeping quiet about my true feelings but then I told her about the voices that were coming out of the plugs which kept telling me I was barren.

She asked me about my life and I told her in a fast-paced monotonous tone all about the curse, about Daddy dying and Toby dying and the Dog dying and the Corbeaux and the Churile and all my dead babies. I told her about Anna and how she'd stolen Michael away from me. But then I got confused and couldn't remember if it was Martha who had stolen Michael away from me or Anna, so I abruptly stopped talking. I looked out the window, the sky was cloudless and I got distracted by a low flying aeroplane and a flock of black birds. The doctor noted all I told her, in her large note pad. Then she asked me more questions, about whether I had any insight into what was wrong with me and whether I felt oriented in time and place. I didn't really understand what she was asking but I was fascinated by the way her nose looked so much like a spout-like beak.

"Doctor you really look like a crow, with your dark beady eyes and your beak-like nose, has anyone ever told you, you look like a crow" I said as fast as I could.

The doctor looked uneasy, she stood up and looked like she would leave, but then she sat down again and began writing in her note pad.

"Answer me", I demanded "it's rude to ignore my legitimate question" I shouted.

The doctor looked at me and calmly asked "do you have any suicidal ideation?"

I looked at her, she really was pitiful, I began to smile at her, she really was unattractive, ugly in fact, her beak looked like it was expanding like Pinocchio's nose.

"Doctor" I said "if you want to know if I have ever considered suicide, why don't you ask me in plain English, instead of saying… suicidal ideation. No, I haven't had suicidal ideation, but to be honest I would quite understand if you had suicidal ideation, as you look like a black crow with a beak and don't let me get started on that frizz you call hair, you're a doctor for God's sake, take some pride in yourself girl".

The doctor looked flustered and began trying to smooth her hair. She got up and stammered that she would visit me once a week and she did.

A few weeks later she told me her diagnosis, I had

confused thinking, there was some evidence of auditory and possibly visual hallucinations and paranoia and a lack of insight.

I felt numb, wrung dry of emotion, as the doctor painted me the sad picture of what my life had become. She outlined my treatment plan of anti-psychotic and mood stabilising medication, psychology sessions and occupational therapy. She asked me if I understood why I had to stay in hospital and after some consideration, I told her that I needed time to rest my brain and get away from the pressures of life.

Days turned into weeks, weeks into months, life turned into one long blur. I felt like I had been trapped, a silly joke gone wrong. I didn't belong here, I wasn't insane but I was surrounded by very mentally ill patients. Around me patients sat slumped in uncomfortable seats, their eyes blank stares, their jaws slack and dribbling. On the other spectrum, some patients presented with aggression and violence, I tried to keep out of their way. One lady named Jenny often responded to internal stimuli, she whispered to herself constantly, sometimes laughing to herself and shouting out. One day she wore her knickers over her head, looking out through the holes meant for legs.

There was one man who seemed very sane. At first, I thought he was a doctor. He was very smart and well presented. He told me he was a professor; his name was David. He explained that he was nearly ready to be discharged, after six months of treatment. He said he was very grateful to feel whole again. He spoke about his search for answers to everything, his unquenching quest for knowledge. He surmised that he had stuffed his brain so full, that one day it all exploded and all the facts he once knew, got all muddled up and overwhelmed him.

On the day he got discharged he came to say goodbye to me, he parted by saying "I often think about the synchronicity of life". I wasn't quite sure what it meant.

The doctor as promised continued to visit me, she said I had suffered a serious episode of depression due to the circumstances of my life and that I seemed to have some paranoid ideation, about Ravens and Corbeaux. There was also she said, fixed ideas about She-Devils, and cow hooves. But more particularly she said, I had a strong and tangible belief that a Churile had stolen my babies by trickery.

I tried to explain to the doctor that these things were real. She watched me with intense interest as I tried to explain how my family had been cursed. She made vigorous notes in her file.

A few months later, after one session, she said I would be allowed visitors soon.

The first to visit was Mum and Mr Alberto, Mum brought me curried goat, rice and salad. The peppery curry sauce was thickened with potatoes softened to a paste and the satisfaction of the meal, made me remember happier times. I devoured the food. Mr Alberto watched me with pitying eyes, while Mum told me about her three trips to London. It seemed Ben had sent them plane tickets quite often. Mum talked about the Tate gallery and the London eye. Mr Alberto said he loved Hampton Court and the lovely wooden furniture. Mum said they got lost in the maze of the garden there.

Mum and Mr Alberto came to visit often and I always looked forward to the food Mum brought with her.

A few months later Martha visited, she hadn't aged

much except that childbirth had thickened her hips. She looked around at the ward clearly distressed. "Oh, Connie" she gasped "I'm going to talk to Ben, you don't belong in a place like this". She told me about the twins, they were starting nursery school soon and she and Michael had gone shopping to buy their uniforms. It was obvious Michael had not told her anything, she was oblivious to the past and I was grateful for that.

She had started her own business making carnival costumes and she was so busy she had to employ a couple of machinists. She told me how well the garage business was doing, Michael's Dad had retired and Michael was now running the garage on his own. Things were going well for them.

Each time she mentioned Michael's name, I felt like a hand opened my ribs and twisted my heart. The pain of the past and what could have been was almost unbearable but I kept a smile painted on my face, like a clown at the circus. Martha was in a happy place and I was pleased for my friend, albeit her happiness slapped me hard.

One time Ruby and Preston came to visit. They had two children, two boys. Ruby said that Preston had got her a personal trainer after each birth. She giggled "I just pinged back into shape". Preston hung on her every word, he was still besotted with her I noted with disappointment. Preston said he now ran an advertising agency and that Ruby featured in some of the adverts. At this Ruby pouted her lips and flickered her hair. My hatred of her re-emerged, thick and fast.

On the radio, Leo Sayer was singing, Ruby turned to me throwing her head back dramatically "remember how we loved this song when we were young?" she said wistfully.

I recalled a joyful day on the beach, which seemed a lifetime ago.

Ruby continued looking at me with a blank gaze "I should have realised you would end up in a place like this, Connie, you always were so intense and strange, you never knew how to relax. Thank God you never had children, imagine a poor child having to visit you here, in this mad house".

Her words were a loaded gun pointed straight at my heart.

"Ruby" I responded coldly "don't feel obliged to visit me again".

I watched as Ruby and Preston walked out of the ward hand in hand, her red heels click clackety on the polished floors.

An intense sadness washed over me and silent salty tears flowed freely down my face. I watched as it made a puddle at my feet.

Chapter 30

Time passed, my therapy sessions continued and in the light of day I saw a vision from the past enter the ward. Tall and handsome, Ben walked in and memories of a past life flooded back. He held my hand warm and strong. He was over from England on holiday with Sarah and the children. His girl was called Serena after Mum, his boy was called Toby after our brother. They were staying with Mum and Mr Alberto.

Ben seemed just the same, except he now spoke with an English accent. He told me that Mum was completely off the booze and had been teetotal for years. He had taken his family to visit Gran and she seemed well. "She's old and fragile" Ben smiled "but she's changed Connie, she's full of regret". He chuckled "do you know Connie I think she's mellowed, she took me aside and apologised to me, for how she treated me, she brought me to tears". He looked away, emotion welling up in him.

"She's got a little dog for company" he continued "a pug, she calls it Bandit, she takes him on walks around the block every day, just to keep herself active. She seems to have found her emotions and a little empathy, through the love of that dog".

He is silent for a while, lost in his own thoughts and I remain passive drinking in the information. He starts to talk again. "Mr Sookoo still looks in on her every day. You know, Connie, I think Gran will die a peaceful death on her porch, swaying on her rocking chair, with that little pug at her feet".

We chat easily until the conversation runs out of steam. Suddenly Ben looks around and says, "Connie, you have to stop this ridiculous talk about She-Devils and vultures if you ever want to get out of this place".

"Ben" I say disappointed fighting back tears,"you have been with me all the way on this journey, you know as well I do that our family is cursed".

Ben strenuously disagreed. He didn't think our family was cursed, so I tried to explain things, so he could see events the way I did. It was good to off load onto Ben to put into words our shared childhood memories, to churn through the painful past together hand in hand.

I explained that Daddy got a mysterious illness and died a horrible death, that Mum became an alcoholic, that we had to live with Gran and the problems of that. I went on to outline Bandit hanging from the stairs, and Toby dying suddenly after a tragic accident involving a Corbeau.

Ben listens, he fidgets but he doesn't interrupt, I continue, "and what about me, a Churile stole my babies and made me childless, my relationships failed and now I am classified as a mad woman. All my dreams and hopes have been dashed". After I finish it feels good to verbalise all these thoughts, good to get them out of me to someone other than a doctor or therapist.

Ben was silent and thoughtful for a while, then he said "Connie, have you ever heard of Occams razor? That when you have competing hypotheses, the one with the fewest assumptions should be selected. So, in other words the simplest explanation is usually the better or right explanation. Ok so Dad getting ill was unexplained but doctors haven't discovered every illness or disease, perhaps if we contact the hospital now, they may have discovered what he died from. Regarding Mum, do you know how many people turn to alcohol when life is difficult? And Bandit died because his lead was too long.

Toby died, Connie, due to a tragic accident - accidents happen every day".

"But, Ben" I insisted my voice raising, "what about my babies and my illness don't you see it's too much tragedy for one family, it's not natural" I felt deflated that Ben didn't seem to understand.

Ben looked exasperated, he looked at Betty sitting nearby slumped in the chair, her eyes unfocussed, staring, spittle dribbling from her mouth. Ben got up abruptly he pointed at Betty "if you keep talking this shit, that's how you are going to end up?"

In desperation, I shouted at him "and Ben what about you?"

"What about me?" Ben answered flatly "I don't feel cursed I'm blessed I have a lovely wife, kids, home, job and life! Even when life was at its toughest, I dusted myself down and carried on, I always see the bright side of life, always ready to carry on regardless. Do you remember what Dad used to say, if at first you don't succeed try and try again. Connie life is always going to throw bitter lemons at you, it's your job to try to make something resembling lemonade".

Ben looked away I could see he was ready to leave, I looked around furtively making sure no-one could hear what I was about to say "yes Ben" I hissed "blah blah blah, don't forget you're a murderer!"

Ben looked unsteady on his feet, he sat down again heavily, he looked at me, a blank unbelieving stare. "Connie" he whispered, "you have really lost the plot".

"No Ben it's you that's lost the plot, I smirked bitterly "don't you remember poor Selassi?"

Ben blinked, the black pupils of his eyes wide with

realisation, he looked like a wounded animal, caught in the headlights. Ben whispered "Connie, I did that to protect you and anyway Selassi walked out of our house on his own two feet".

Ben looked around the ward and then back at me with a look of pure disgust.

"I'm done" he muttered. As he walked out of the ward, my bitter laugh followed him down the corridor.

Weeks passed and I had no more visitors. On another nameless, mind numbing day, a nurse came to give me my medication. She smiled kindly and said, "your brother seems nice, he's trying to get you out of here". She paused for a while and continued. "Sometimes in life, you need to play the game. I know you believe your family was cursed, but maybe keep that to yourself, and stop with all the She-devil and Corbeau stuff and maybe, just maybe you will get out of this dump".

A few days after this Ben came again. When I saw him walking towards me my stomach turned to jelly, I was a nervous wreck. I knew I had wounded him, which was my intention at the time, but now I regretted it. Deep down I knew Ben was the one person I could always depend on all my life. He sat opposite me, he was pleasant, I could sense no hint of ill feelings towards me. I was relieved.

He said he found a twenty-four-hour supported accommodation for me which, was part funded by the government. He would fund the rest. He had spoken to the doctors and they would be willing to discharge me, if I gained some insight into my illness and if my delusions subsided. As Ben was talking, Jenny came to sit near to us, she had her panties over her trousers. "I have got to protect myself" she whispered to Ben, "they are coming to rape me". Then she began whispering to herself.

Ben looked at me incredulous he barked "Jesus Christ, Connie you need to get out of here!"

The next time Ben came back, I apologised to him for calling him a murderer and I tried to explain to him how I genuinely felt.

"Ben" I said "over the years I have lost everything, this isn't the life I imagined for myself at all, I seem to hurt and reject people but in the end the person I end up hurting is myself. I have lost sight of what's important in life".

Ben looked around the ward, he didn't say anything to me for a while. Then he responded "you must let the past go, Connie, fate is not outside your control. Fate is what you make it, you can change it if you want, through perseverance. You always think of the future as set in stone, as something predetermined, but I always think of the future as fluid".

He paused and shifted in the chair "think of your future as fluid, full of possibilities, take back control of your life, Connie" he smiled.

Chapter 31

It took another four months but I was eventually discharged to the place Ben had found for me. The accommodation was small and functional but it was mine. I was on a care in the community programme and they set me up with a part time job, working in the kitchen at Servol life Centre. It was a Catholic institution that provided training programmes for young people.

The job was easy, I didn't have to think too much, all I had to do was smile and be sociable as I served food. I found to my surprise that I was good at talking and interacting with others, something that hadn't really come easily to me in the past.

It was here I met James a tutor for Servol. He taught Art and was always friendly to me as I served him his food. I came to look forward to seeing him and the easy banter we shared. One-day James asked me to have coffee with him in the canteen. Initially I was nervous and awkward but he put me at my ease as he asked me for a favour. "Connie" he said in his gentle way "you have an open and interesting face; would you mind posing for me so I can do your portrait".

That evening I went home and looked at myself in the mirror, I wasn't really pretty but I was attractive and did have an open and honest face. The fine lines around my eyes and chin aged me, like the circles on the bark of a tree, they were the markers of the contours of my life.

After some thought, I agreed to model for James and that's how our relationship started. What I had with James was different to what I had known before. It wasn't the intensity of the love I had felt with Michael, or the hopeful perfection I had sought with Nick. What I found with James was like slipping on an old comfortable cardigan and wrapping myself up in the warmth and snugness of it, marvelling at the way it fitted me so well. I realised that true love was not the breathless excitement of passion. Love, I came to understand in slow increments, was the connection and sharing of souls, a calm completeness running from my head to my toes.

In small chunks, I told James in painful detail all about my life, the curse, the Corbeau, the Churile, my babies that I couldn't hold onto, my mental illness and the medication I had to take to keep me well. He listened patiently, never judging me or interrupting. It soothed me to talk, to visualise the words oozing out the reality of my life. James did not have answers or explanations for all that had occurred but he said he could feel the truth of my words through my tears. He said he could tell that my sorrow and hurt had worn away at me, exposing the fabric of my frayed being. James made me realise that I needed to mend the frays to become whole again. I really believe that his love healed what was broken in me. Over time his complete support and understanding, filled the gaps in me, that I hadn't realised needed filling.

James encouraged me to paint the experiences of my life in vivid colours, to unlock all my turmoil in a palette of hues. I found that doing so was more therapeutic than anything provided on Petal Ward. I painted a picture of a tree, a mix of vibrant and metallic colours with many branches, representing the many aspects and people in my life, lost and present. It was sort of abstract, willowy and hazy, but clear to me. James said it was good. I was more critical.

"I'm not sure about it" I said "it's not perfect, I might paint it again" I confessed to James.

"It doesn't need to be perfect" James said wisely "it's the imperfections that paint the perfect story".

My tree of life now hangs proudly in the living room, James had it framed and mounted and a little brass plaque is pinned on the front of the frame.

The plaque reads - 'The Perfect Imperfections of a Life – by Connie Costello'.

It is with regret that I must admit, that I had a few hiccups along the way and had to be readmitted to Petal Ward. But with James by my side with his comforting support, the admissions were short and I was discharged quickly back to his care. James was my safety blanket, he gave me the freedom to be myself.

Ben sent tickets for us to visit him in England and we went a couple of times. James loved to travel and it was heart-warming spending time with Ben, Sarah and my niece and nephew. We visited all the tourist attractions Mum had told me about, like Big Ben and the London eye. James oozed contented satisfaction as we visited art galleries. He busily sketched everything in sight. I marvelled as I found myself laughing and relaxing. A new carefree world bloomed and was revealed to me. James and I had captured a good simple life. It was free of impatience and the complexities of striving for perfection. The monotony of everyday life was steady and comforting.

My favourite time of all, was when we packed up the car for the weekend and headed for the little beach house, James had inherited. Here I really feel alive, surrounded by nature and the unspoilt beauty of the sea. We'd sit on the beach for hours both with our easels, painting easily, no words needed. Safe in our silence, my private memories meandering softly in my head.

One day I turn to James and say "James, my love, for a long time I felt my life was cursed. But now I feel so lucky to have found you. Finally, I am at peace, I feel I belong, I feel complete. It's funny I feel my life has turned full circle. Now I feel blessed not cursed".

I look at him long and deep and I smile "you saved me James".

James reaches for my hand and kisses my fingers "no Connie" he grins "you saved yourself, I just showed you the way".

"I wish I met you years ago, James. I wasted so much time and life's so short" I sigh.

James looks at me in his calming way "we found happiness Connie, that's all that matters, the timing of when we found it is not important".

We sit silent again, content. There are specks of sparkles floating in the sunbeam above. I think of childhood and laughter and ice-cream with sparkles and hundreds and thousands. The wind invisible and weightless, feels light-hearted and free as it blows our thoughts calm and clear. The nerves in my head feel smooth and straight and ordered. We watch the white sands, the waves rising and falling, the tide comes in.

Then we stand, arms linked, until the sun sets in the horizon. Another perfect day in an imperfect life.

Chapter 32

The end is near, I can feel it. I am slipping away further from this world and into whatever world awaits me. I'm not sure of anything now, is there another world after this one. My mind is fuzzy, full of thoughts and memories, competing with each other for my attention, but I can't join up the dots.

I can sense people around my bed, relatives perhaps, people who knew me when I was Connie Costello.

My head feels confused, am I still Connie Costello now I wonder? Or is that who I used to be? I can't recall. I remember Connie Costello as a young girl, who had dreams of a perfect life. But someone put a curse on her family and her life was far from perfect. Did I have a good life, even though it was imperfect? Is that even possible? I try to think but my head hurts.

I slip away into oblivion and then I wake again. I force my eyes open and I am astonished to see Mum, Dad and Toby sitting at the end of my bed, bathed in golden sunshine. Mum looks radiant, Dad smiles, his perfect white teeth on show and Toby grins at me with that cheeky little face of his. I feel jubilant; my heart wants to burst with joy. Mum reaches out towards me, she smiles and says "Connie, we've come to take you home".

I slip into oblivion again but then I awake with a sense of panic, a need to take action. A nurse comes in and briskly fusses about my bed. As she is about to leave, I tug urgently at her arm.

"What is it Connie" she says kindly.

I try to speak but I am so weak. "What is it dear?" she says louder close to my ear.

I summon all the strength I can muster and murmur "priest".

"Do you want a priest dear?" she says but she does not wait for an answer and hurries away. I can hardly see her, my vision is blurred. I slip away into oblivion again.

I feel a finger on my head, making the sign of the cross, but I'm too weak and I slip away again.

Suddenly I'm awake again but I can't open my eyes, I can hear the 23rd Psalm being read – "The Lord is my shepherd, I shall not want".

I want desperately to listen but everything is a blur.

I can hear the words being spoken but I don't comprehend them at all, as I slip away.

Suddenly my body seems weightless and consumed by a warm feeling of calm. My head feels all ordered now as though someone has brushed all the nerves in my head straight and neat.

A bright light races towards me and beckons me - I'm being lifted and pulled towards an all encompassing shimmering glow...

I can hear the priest again - "and I shall dwell in the house of the Lord forever and ever, Amen".

Chapter 33

Sam Ramlochan was dying. He was being eaten up inside and he could feel it chewing away.

The cancer had almost consumed him and it was time to depart this world. He wondered if there was an afterlife, or if this was it, one innings and out!

He always wondered if the cancer was punishment for the one really evil thing he did in his life. He'd blanked it out of his mind for years, but now that he was ill, those memories came drifting back, like an old video rewinding, slowly back to that point he'd thought he'd permanently erased.

The tape played back in the dusty corner of his mind...

Sam approached the witch doctor - rumour had it he was the best Obeah Man in the country. He lived down a creek frequented more by crabs than people. Sam was shocked to see the witch doctor, he hadn't really thought about what he was expecting but this man was as black as tar and his hair and teeth as white as snow. He looked ancient as though he'd been on the earth for centuries. His back was bent over almost double with the strain of what seemed, too much time on earth. Ironically, he had an open kind face which was lined and creased like a shiny black prune. When he spoke the witch doctor's voice was gentle and he spoke with an all surpassing wisdom. Sam recalled thinking that the old man was the conduit rather than the source of the evil.

He'd asked the witch doctor to cast the strongest spell he could, on his tenant Harry Costello. The witch doctor had asked him twice if he was sure, as there were other milder curses he could cast. But Sam Ramlochan was adamant he wanted the strongest spell to be cast. His pride had been hurt and *that man* needed to be punished. So he confirmed his instructions, that the curse should be as bad as possible.

The witch doctor turned to the shelves of his hut that were lined with books - he reached the top shelf, which seemed to be strained and bowed with the weight of the load above it. The witch doctor opened the largest book and Sam noticed that the pages seemed yellowed by centuries of time passing.

The witch doctor turned to Sam and said that sometimes a curse that was cast, was too powerful for one man to bear and that the curse sometimes transferred to other family members as well.

Sam recalled he was mad with rage, he was so damned vexed, he didn't care less if the curse transferred on to others, as long as *that man* got what was coming to him.

Before Sam had left the witch doctor's hut, the witch doctor had asked "what afflictions do you want to be cast?"

Sam remembered feeling perplexed by the question "and asked "what do you mean?"

The witch doctor sighed a deep wheezy sigh "there are different types of afflictions you can request - pain, suffering, physical sickness, mental sickness, hardship, difficult life and even death. Which of these do you want?"

Sam remembered his instantaneous answer "all of the above".

The witch doctor turned the pages of the book which seemed to be whispering and imparting past secrets, held together from the end of time. After some time the whispering stopped abruptly and the witch doctor closed the book. He looked up at Sam and said "it's done".

The witch doctor was serene when he bade goodbye to Sam but said in a placid voice which seemed to be filled with warning,

"Remember this, you have entered into a pact with the Devil and he is unpredictable. He can be found in a place at the end of the earth where the sun has been banished and dark forces prevail everlasting".

Sam felt a cold shiver down his spine as he left the hut...

He recalled the day clearly a couple of years later, when his oldest son had come home with the news that Harry Costello had died a horrible painful death. His son had said the nurse who treated Harry at the time of his death, was shocked that Harry had bled profusely from all his orifices. The doctors seemingly had no explanation for Harry's sudden and prolonged illness. The nurse said she had never seen anything so horrific and sad, with his wife and young family crying over him.

Upon hearing the news Sam had felt a pang of deep gut wrenching guilt; he slept fitfully for several weeks before deciding to return to the witch doctor.

Upon seeing Sam at his door again, the witch doctor did not seem surprised. Sam explained that he had made a mistake and that he wanted the curse to be stopped.

Without words the witch doctor returned to the whispering book. Upon consulting the yellowing pages of the book again, the witch doctor said the curse could not be stopped once it had already started. There was a small possibility he said, that if the intended victims had not yet been affected by the curse, then there was a chance that crossing of the oceans might break the spell.

But there was no guarantee.

The witch doctor smiled calmly at Sam, revealing his white teeth in stark contrast to his black skin and Sam immediately realised that the unnatural contrast of teeth and skin, emanated from an unnatural being. The witch doctor opened his mouth and what came out was a ghostly echoey voice. "You made a pact with the Devil, he owns your soul, you lose control".

The witch doctor then broke into a deep booming laughter, which sounded like it was coming from the depths of the earth. When Sam looked up, he saw that an old Hag was standing beside the witch doctor, she was laughing too, a loud toothless evil echo.

Sam left the hut for the second time and felt the contents of his stomach reach his mouth in record time; he steadied himself on the old coconut tree outside and threw up violently. A cold shiver ran down his spine and he began to shake from the cold fear within him. On the way home he vowed to forget about the matter and to never think about it again.

...Sam came back to the present, as the gnawing of the cancer chomped away at him.

In hindsight, the altercation between himself and Harry Costello now seemed so petty and he reflected on why his younger and much unwiser self had taken it all so seriously.

He wondered if the curse had really worked, after all the witch doctor said there was no guarantee. Sam pondered on his whole life, now almost past and he hoped against hope that the curse had not worked. Moments now from death Sam finally (but now far too late) appreciated the true value of life.

Sam believed that all the good things he did in his life, must counterbalance the one really bad thing he did. On balance surely, the good must outweigh the bad.

Sam felt confused; his physical body seemed to be losing definition as though he were becoming an undefined mass of cancer cells. The last thought that popped into his dying brain was *this world is so messed up, heaven and hell is right here on earth!*

As he closed his eyes he could feel a darkness envelope him, dragging him down as he took his last gasp of breath and he was extinguished.

Chapter 34 – Epilogue

Corvid perched at the threshold of the worlds. The world of flesh at one end, the world of spirits at the other. He observes human decay and sees the floaty souls leaving defunct bodies, to enter the spirit world. This is where the dead reside where no physical body is needed. Death sets the soul free, it cannot hear, it cannot see, it cannot think, it has no identity.

It was always so, extending beyond time. But he knows it's not the final destination.

Corvid smiles his crooked smile and flaps his wings, he is a powerful flier, soaring through the worlds, crying out his deep throaty rattling song. His song is a long lamentation, but he has no remorse or sadness. He is carefree, he is Corvid.

He lands in the world of flesh. He looks down at small black shiny patent shoes, he looks up and a little girl meets his gaze. She backs away, horror spreading across her face, she bawls out "Mummy come quick Cobo!"

The mother comes running out, she crouches down to the little girl "what's wrong love" she asks with concern.

The girl sniffles back tears. "There was a big Cobo, it looked like it was going to eat me, it was standing right there!" she screeches.

The mother looks up, the sun is blinding but in the distance an old man walks hurriedly, his head bowed over his stooped shoulders. Then a squawk above startles her and she sees a large black Corbeau flying away.

Acknowledgements

I owe a debt of gratitude to Trinidadian folklore for providing some of the ideas for this book.

Special thanks to Rebecca Alana Lowe and Jay Datta for advising me that dogs go to the same heaven humans go to and not to a separate dog heaven.

Special mention to my school friend Ingrid Persaud who advised me that there is at least one book in all of us, just waiting to be written.

Massive love and thanks to my lovely family and relatives in London and in Trinidad for their encouragement and support.

I am blessed to have a loyal army of friends all of whom have helped and travelled on this book journey with me, they know who they are. Love always.

About the Author

Abigail Weekes-Lowe is of Trinidadian heritage. She was born in London, England. As a teenager she lived in Trinidad W.I. for five years and attended St Joseph's Catholic Convent in Port of Spain. She lives in London with her husband Denis and her daughter Rebecca. Abigail has been a practicing Solicitor since 1991 and has been an Associate Mental Health Act Hospital Manager for the Barnet, Enfield and Haringey Mental Health Trust in London since 1998. She is in a book reading group.

Both the characters and events in the book are fictional, albeit some elements are based on real life events e.g. her father and her family dog both died in the way described in this book. In addition, her favourite Shakespeare play is Macbeth and her favourite piece of classical music is Beethoven's Romance No.2. She also used to sing along to Leo Sayer in her youth.

Available worldwide from

Amazon

30185317R00109

Printed in Great Britain
by Amazon